People probably think I have a lot of secrets. I know a lot of people think of me as a very private, sometimes cold person who doesn't like to reveal what's really going on inside his head. That's partially true, of course. But I don't have a lot of deep, dark secrets. Only one.

I'm scared of regaining my vision. And I don't mean that I'm scared of the surgery or the tests or anything like that. I actually have a lot of faith in doctors. Maybe being blind makes you more trusting of people who are there to help you; I'm not sure.

I'm scared of seeing.

Don't miss any of the books in
Making Out
by Katherine Applegate
from Avon Flare

Coming Soon

MAKING OUT #10

Nina shapes up

KATHERINE APPLEGATE

AN AVON FLARE BOOK

AVON BOOKS, INC.
1350 Avenue of the Americas
New York, New York 10019

Copyright © 1996 by Daniel Weiss Associates, Inc., and Katherine Applegate
Published by arrangement with Daniel Weiss Associates, Inc.
Library of Congress Catalog Card Number: 98-93664
ISBN: 0-380-80743-2
www.avonbooks.com

First Avon Flare Printing: March 1999

AVON FLARE TRADEMARK REG. U.S. PAT. OFF. AND IN OTHER COUNTRIES, MARCA REGISTRADA, HECHO EN U.S.A.

Printed in the U.S.A.

WCD   10   9   8   7   6   5   4   3   2   1

For Michael

Zoey

What is my deepest, darkest secret? I don't have to think too long about that one. Yes, secrets have definitely been on my mind a lot lately. When you think about it, it's pretty strange. I mean, on an island of only three hundred people, where everyone knows each other and most people are friends — _supposed_ to be friends, anyway — you'd think people would know enough not to keep secrets. Or at least they'd know enough not to act in a way that could possibly hurt anyone else.

But it's human nature, I guess. Betrayal, dishonesty — all of those wonderful

1

traits that separate us from plant life. People just have a way of getting into situations that certain other people shouldn't know about. And on Chatham Island, secrets unfortunately have an unnerving habit of becoming public knowledge pretty quickly.

Take my parents, for example. They tried to hide their sordid pasts from each other and, in the process, from my brother, Benjamin, and me. I have to give them credit—they succeeded in keeping the truth hidden a lot longer than most people around here could.

That is, until I happened to walk in on my mom with her old flame. Mr. McRoyan.

Yes, <u>Jake</u>'s dad — Jake, my former boyfriend. Which led to my parents nearly getting divorced. Which led to Benjamin and me discovering we had a possibly insane half sister named Lara McAvoy. Which led to Lara moving in with us....

Anyway.

Another thing about secrets is their consequences, which tend to range from horrible to awful — especially if the people involved are the ones you care about most.

So back to the question. What is my deepest, darkest secret? For a while I tried not to have any secrets, because I saw how they hurt people. I suppose I was pretty hard on some of my friends over their secrets. Maybe I even considered myself to be...well, morally superior to a few of them. I'm not going to mention any names, but the tall, beautiful older sister of a certain best friend of mine comes to mind....

I'm still avoiding the question, aren't I?

The truth is, I <u>didn't</u> have any deep, dark secrets until very recently. But that all changed when Aaron Mendel showed up on Chatham Island. Or more specifically, that changed when I decided not to tell anyone about how I've been spending time with him. Or about how I love listening to him play the guitar, or about the way

4

his lips feel against mine....

Ah, yes. Secrets.

I remember an old quote back from the days when I used to collect them and post them on the wall of my dormer. Back in those days, of course, everything was a lot simpler. My home was normal. Lara wasn't sharing a bathroom with me. And the mere thought of being unfaithful to Lucas was enough to make me sick.

The quote was: "You only hurt the ones you love."

Funny how things change, isn't it?

One

I'm in big, big trouble.

Zoey Passmore hunched over the bathroom sink, staring into the face in the mirror. She knew the face to be her own, yet at the same time it seemed completely unrecognizable. It wasn't the dark circles that ringed her blue eyes, nor the rumpled blond hair that looked like some knotted, misshapen wig. She knew she looked terrible because she hadn't slept. But *why* she hadn't slept was another matter.

What was I thinking?

She licked her dry lips, listening to the steady hammering of her heart. She *hadn't* been thinking. Never again, she promised herself. One kiss—okay, a long, sensual kiss, a *deep* kiss, a kiss that took her breath away—but just one. No irreversible damage could have been done with one kiss, right? After all, Lucas *had* kissed Claire. Not only that, he'd wanted a lot more. And Zoey had forgiven him. That had been the end of that. Besides, the moment she saw Lucas on the ferry that morning, any image of Aaron Mendel would be wiped from her memory—

A loud knock on the bathroom door scattered her thoughts.

"What is it?" Zoey asked irritably.

"Oh," said a dull female voice. "Sorry. I didn't think anyone was in there."

Quiet footsteps padded away.

Lara, the light is on, the door is closed, it's seven-fifteen on a school morning, and you didn't think anyone was in here?

Zoey sighed deeply, fighting the urge to say something. She turned on the faucet and splashed some water on her face. The cold liquid felt good against her hot skin. She needed to relax. It wasn't Lara's fault that her life was a mess. It wasn't Lara's fault that as of the previous night, Zoey Passmore could easily win the title of World's Biggest Hypocrite.

After hastily pulling on some jeans and a plain wool sweater that Lucas loved, she headed downstairs. A violin concerto was pouring out of Benjamin's room, filling the house with its sweet, rich sound. The soothing music reassured her. *Everything will be fine*, she told herself as she walked past her brother's door. She just had to act normal. That was the key. As long as she acted normal, she could put the previous night behind her, right?

"Hey, where were you last night?" Benjamin asked over the music.

Zoey frowned. Good old Benjamin. He was sitting on the edge of his bed, grinning slightly behind his ever-present dark glasses.

"What do you mean?" she asked. "I was here."

"Around nine o'clock?" he prodded.

Zoey bit her lip. "I told you. I was up at the Grays' house, looking for Eesh." At least that was *partially* true. She had been up at Aisha's parents' bed-and-breakfast—but she hadn't been looking for Aisha. "Why?" she added, for good measure.

His grin widened. "Eesh was here with Nina and me," he said. "Remember?"

"Then I guess I should have stayed home," she grumbled. She knew Benjamin was just teasing her, but she couldn't help feeling a little nervous. He would never suspect the truth, would he? Then again, nobody was as perceptive as her older brother. Had he picked up on some offhand remark she'd made when she'd gotten home?

Zoey shook her head. It was only quarter past seven, and already she was paranoid and half out of her mind from lack of sleep. Nobody could possibly know about her kiss. *Nobody*.

"You guys?" Lara called.

"Oh, boy," Zoey mumbled, trying not to roll her eyes. Lara was coming down the stairs. She was wearing the most ridiculous polka-dot pajamas Zoey had ever seen. Her brown hair was sticking out in a thousand different directions—like an explosion in a mattress factory, as Nina Geiger would say. Lara looked as if *she* were the one who had stayed up all night. Then again, that wasn't such a far-fetched possibility.

"Hey." Lara poked her head over Zoey's shoulder into Benjamin's room. Her breath reeked of too much toothpaste. "Look, I was just wondering if you could maybe turn the music down a little bit. I can hear it in my room, and I kinda wanted to go back to sleep. . . ."

"Hey, no problem. My fault." Benjamin reached over to his stereo and turned down the volume, then snatched *The Short Stories of Ernest Hemingway* off the floor and held it up to his face. The book was

8

upside-down. "I need to do some last-minute cramming before the English quiz today, anyway."

After a few seconds of silence, Lara forced an awkward laugh. "Uh-huh . . . yeah," she muttered. "Thanks." She turned and hurried back up the stairs.

Benjamin lowered the book, his smile intact.

Normally Zoey would have smiled back conspiratorially. Benjamin's quirky sense of humor about his blindness had a way of making people who didn't know him uncomfortable. It was his way of sharing something with those he trusted and distancing himself from those he didn't. And like Zoey, he definitely didn't trust Lara.

"Come on, you guys, let's eat!" her father yelled from the kitchen. "You don't want to miss the ferry."

The ferry. Zoey's heart skipped a beat. Everyone would be on that ferry. Nina, who would ask her all about why she hadn't been home until late the night before—on a Wednesday night, a *school* night. And Aisha, who would more than likely do the same.

And of course Lucas, who would hear the two of them asking and begin to wonder why Zoey had suddenly developed a stutter and a tendency to blush for no apparent reason.

"Where is she?" Lucas Cabral wondered out loud. He was standing on the deck behind his house, leaning over the railing, gazing down the hill into the window of the brightly lit Passmore kitchen.

He shivered. It looked so warm and cozy in there.

The sun was just emerging over the crisp blue horizon, and the air was freezing—probably no more than twenty degrees. He glanced at his watch. Seventy-twenty. He had to be going soon if he was going to

9

make the seven-forty ferry. Had Zoey decided to skip breakfast for some reason? Both Mr. and Mrs. Passmore were sitting in the breakfast nook with their backs to him, but Zoey had yet to appear.

"There she is."

The words made icy clouds as he spoke them. Zoey and Benjamin were coming into the kitchen now. For a moment Lucas forgot about the weather. Zoey was wearing one of his favorite outfits—a fuzzy wool sweater that perfectly complemented her blond hair. Not to mention certain other prominent features. . . .

He laughed suddenly. *Pathetic*. That was the word that came to mind, but it didn't even come close to describing what he probably looked like—squinting through his neighbor's window in his winter parka and black knit cap, with his long blond hair hanging in his eyes. *Perverted* was more like it.

But he couldn't help himself. Not a morning had gone by during the past month when he hadn't felt divinely blessed that Zoey had forgiven him for his idiotic little mistake with Claire. Even now, just thinking of how he'd cheated on Zoey made him cringe. With *Claire*, no less—the ice princess herself.

Well, he'd learned to keep his hormones in check since then. Or he'd learned to *try* to keep them in check, anyway—which was about the best any self-respecting male could do. That was one of the reasons he made himself go through with this little ritual: to stare down at Zoey—in rain or snow or blizzard or typhoon—and remind himself that, yes, there really was more to life than getting laid.

How many other guys were as lucky as he was? Some guys were separated from the girls they loved by thousands of miles. All he had to do was walk out on his back porch to see Zoey smiling up at him.

Well, *usually* smiling up at him. That morning she hadn't even so much as glanced out the back window. Strange. She obviously had something on her mind. Come to think of it, something *had* been bothering her all week, but she hadn't wanted to talk about it. And when he'd gone down to look for her the night before, she hadn't been there . . .

A brief, unpleasantly hot sensation flashed through his body. He knew the feeling well. Suspicion. He immediately hated himself for it. But, like his hormones, it was another thing he couldn't quite control. Actually, hormones and suspicion went hand in hand. The last time he'd gotten suspicious of Zoey, he'd wound up in the backseat of Claire's father's Mercedes. Suspicion hadn't exactly worked wonders for him.

He shook his head.

He was the dog—not Zoey.

Sighing, he turned and headed back inside. If something was bothering her, he'd find out about it on the ferry.

Two

Nina Geiger hated the ferry ride to school in the winter. Everybody had to crowd into the little room below deck, suffocating in a stagnant cloud of their own morning breath for the half hour it took to reach Weymouth.

"I think I'm going to stay up here," Claire announced as Nina headed for the ferry's narrow stairwell.

"Uh, Claire," Nina began, pulling the hood of her jacket tightly over her head. "I know vampires live forever and all, but even *you* could freeze to death up here."

"I'll be fine," Claire said, smiling her wintry smile in spite of Nina's barb. She gestured across the deck toward the horizon opposite the mainland. "There are some cirrus clouds coming in from the east. You know, when the clouds look like that, like pulled cotton, it's a pretty good sign that there may be some precipitation—"

"Suit yourself," Nina said quickly, turning down the stairs. It was way too cold for a twenty-minute discourse on meteorology. What was with Claire that day? Getting worked up over a few wispy clouds was normal for her. But Claire seldom smiled before the sun was down, and she'd been acting disgustingly pleased with herself all morning.

"Hey, there," a voice behind her called.

As soon as Nina saw Benjamin entering the cabin, all thoughts of Claire vanished. He grinned impishly. "Come sit next to me."

Nina smiled and slid onto the bench beside him, hardly noticing that Lucas and Zoey were there, too. Benjamin was truly amazing. How could he tell it was her just by the way she entered a room?

"So how's it going, Eesh?" he asked.

"Very funny," Nina said, slipping her hand into his.

"Hey," he whispered, squeezing her fingers. "We can't let Nina see this. She'd fly into a jealous rage."

Nina tried to fight the blush creeping up her neck. The previous night had been one of the most embarrassing experiences of her life. She'd come bursting into Benjamin's room, convinced he and Aisha were in the midst of a hot and heavy make-out session.

She cast a flustered glance at Zoey and Lucas, who were sitting on the bench across from her. Lucas had a look of amusement on his face, but for some reason Zoey looked as if the morning banter was making her seriously ill.

"So you thought Eesh and Benjamin were doing the nasty behind your back?" Lucas said.

Nina stuck out her tongue at him.

"I know all about it," he added with a sly grin.

"And how's that?" Nina asked.

"I got this deranged call from Christopher last night at about one A.M. He said he was positive that Eesh was cheating on him. With Benjamin."

13

"Uh-oh," Benjamin muttered.

"Well, the thought never crossed *my* mind," Nina stated. "I'm too mature for such juvenile pangs of jealousy."

Lucas rolled his eyes.

Actually, Nina really *had* thought that Benjamin was fooling around with Aisha behind her back. The notion was insane, of course, and in light of what she had learned, it made her feel like the most immature, self-centered brat on the planet.

Because the night before—*after* Nina had made a total fool out of herself—Benjamin had told her why he and Asiha had been spending so much time together. Aisha had been helping Benjamin use the Internet to find information about a new surgical procedure at Boston General Hospital that could possibly restore his sight.

Restore his sight.

The words still had an unreal, dreamlike quality. The idea itself was along the same lines as world peace—impossible, beyond imagining. Benjamin had told her that the chances were slim. Apparently the doctors were optimistic, but he still had to go to Boston and have some tests done. He wasn't sure when or even *if* he was going to go through with it. That's why he was insisting on keeping the whole thing secret—even from Zoey. *Especially* from Zoey.

Nina's eyes flashed to her best friend, who was staring blankly at the cold metal floor. Keeping secrets from either of the Passmore siblings was definitely *not* Nina's forte.

"So where were you last night, anyway?" Nina asked, hoping to distract herself temporarily. She fished through her jacket pocket for her pack of Lucky

Strikes and shoved a cigarette between her lips, not bothering to light it.

Zoey's unblinking eyes remained fixed to the floor.

"Earth to Zoey, Earth to Zoey." Nina cupped her hands around her mouth, imitating the sound of a walkie-talkie. "Mayday, Mayday. We've lost all contact."

"Huh?" Zoey asked, looking up. "Oh." She shook her head, avoiding Nina's gaze. "I was looking for Eesh." The words sounded oddly flat, as if they'd been rehearsed.

"A likely story." Nina raised her eyebrows at Lucas.

Lucas just shrugged.

Zoey jumped to her feet. "Speaking of Eesh, I think I'm gonna go upstairs and wait for her," she said distractedly. "She's late, as usual. Somebody's gotta tell Skipper Too to wait in case she misses . . ."

Her voice trailed into silence as her footsteps clattered up the stairs.

Skipper Too was everyone's nickname for Tom Clement, the captain of the *Island Breeze*, nicknamed the *Minnow*—all in honor of *Gilligan's Island* reruns. Skipper Too was punctual to the point of being anal—in Nina's opinion, anyway. She frowned at Lucas. "Um, math isn't my strongest subject, but I calculate the odds of Skipper Too's waiting for Eesh to be about one in eight zillion. What's with her?"

"Beats me," Lucas said, looking at Benjamin. "She *was* up at the Grays' looking for Eesh last night, wasn't she?"

"That's what she told me," Benjamin replied.

Lucas shook his head. "Why is it that all women are insane?" he mumbled. "Maybe I should go up

15

there and see—'' He broke off as some heavy L.L. Bean boots lumbered down the stairs.

Jake McRoyan walked into the cabin. His Red Sox cap was pulled so far down over his head that it nearly covered his eyes. ''Damn, it's cold out there,'' he said to nobody in particular. He glanced around, then sat with obvious reluctance next to Lucas.

''You want to know why women are insane, Lucas?'' Nina asked, taking a deep drag of her unlit cigarette. She let the air in her lungs out slowly and gave Jake a big, fake smile. ''Take a look at some of the men in the world.''

''Up yours, *Ninny*,'' Jake said, smiling back.

''Original line, *Joke*,'' Nina retorted.

Lucas just kept looking at Benjamin. ''You think I should go up there?''

Benjamin laughed lightly. ''Don't you know the laws of the Passmore household, Lucas?'' He slipped his arm under Nina's. ''Zoey doesn't get involved with my relationships, and I don't get involved with hers.''

''Thanks a lot, man,'' Lucas grumbled, staring at the stairs. ''You're a real pal.''

Nina leaned back on the bench. *She* would find out whatever was bothering Zoey—not that she would tell Lucas. Poor guy. He was a definite improvement over Jake, but still . . . she didn't exactly envy her best friend. She sighed, luxuriating in the feeling of Benjamin's overcoat snuggled against her own. Who would have thought that of all her friends, she would have the most stable love life?

''Trust me, Lucas,'' she said, ''you wouldn't want to go up there. Unless you want to hear Claire's fascinating lecture about today's forecast.''

Claire Geiger smiled as Zoey strolled over to the railing beside her. "Too crowded for you downstairs?" she asked.

"I just needed some fresh air," Zoey said quietly. She stared across the bay toward Weymouth.

Well, well. That's a little odd, isn't it? Claire suppressed a smile. Zoey, probably more than anyone, considered all the island kids to be one big cozy family. It didn't even matter that most of them had been romantically involved with each other at one time or another. There was nothing to hide.

But now the situation was a little different.

Zoey "I'm-the-perfect-girlfriend" Passmore was no longer Chatham Island's shining example of monogamy. And Claire was the only one who knew it.

Admittedly, Claire hadn't been thrilled when she'd seen Aaron and Zoey making out the night before, but her initial unhappiness had quickly faded. After careful reflection, Claire had realized that she could use this knowledge to her advantage. She hadn't quite yet figured out how, but she would. She always did.

The net result, of course, would be that Zoey would return to Lucas—which was for the best, anyway. And Aaron, in his better judgment, would come running to *her*.

After a long horn blast, the ferry began inching away from the dock. Claire shook her head. "Looks like Eesh is going to have to take the water taxi."

"Yeah, for some reason cold weather makes Eesh even later than usual," Zoey said absently. Her teeth were chattering now. She wrapped her arms around herself, struggling to keep warm.

Claire nodded. Out of the corner of her eye, she

scrutinized Zoey's faraway expression. Zoey didn't seem overly guarded or nervous. Good. That meant she had no idea that Claire knew. No—it was better than good. It was *perfect*. Zoey believed her little make-out session with Aaron Mendel was a secret. And she would never suspect otherwise.

Claire allowed herself a little grin. "So, have you started your paper on *The Scarlet Letter* yet?" she asked.

Zoey shook her head, keeping her eyes fixed on the mainland. "I haven't even finished the book. Maybe I'll just rent the movie tonight."

Claire shook her head. "Demi Moore doesn't do Hester Prynne justice. The book is much better. Anyway, the movie's ending is different."

"Oh, well." Zoey shrugged, clearly not interested in pursuing the conversation.

"I actually had fun writing the paper—if you can believe it," Claire said in as relaxed a voice as she could manage. She paused. "Adultery is such an interesting topic, don't you think?"

Zoey's head whipped around. "No, I don't." Her eyes bored into Claire's.

"Oh," Claire said nonchalantly. *Easy, there*. That little jab hadn't been so smart. Zoey's unflinching stare was growing colder by the second. "Something wrong?"

"No." Zoey's eyes narrowed. "Why?"

Claire shrugged. "You just look like a little preoccupied. Not to mention tired."

Zoey's mouth curved downward slightly. "Yeah, well, I didn't sleep so well last night. I guess I'm still getting used to having a new sister around." She turned back toward the bay.

"How's that going, by the way?"

Zoey pursed her lips. "It's going."

"The island does seem to have gotten a little more crowded in the past month, hasn't it?" Claire said.

"I guess it has."

"After all, the way things are looking right now between my dad and Sarah Mendel, I could get a new sibling myself." Claire hesitated. "A cute one, I might add."

"Oh, yeah." Zoey swallowed. "That guy Aaron."

That guy Aaron! Claire almost shook her head. It was nice to see Zoey sweat a little, but she still couldn't help feeling sorry for her. Zoey had a lot to learn about keeping skeletons safely locked in the closet.

Three

Benjamin stood outside one of the side doors of the school building, trying to avoid the cold bite of the winter breeze and the rush of students swarming past him. He couldn't believe that classes were actually over. For the first time in a long, long while, he hadn't been able to concentrate. Intense concentration had become second nature; it was a necessity to compensate for his blindness. But that day his instinctive ability to focus seemed to be eluding him. As a result, the day had dragged on endlessly—and everything had eventually just melted together in a fuzzy mush.

At least he'd avoided Zoey and Claire.

He wasn't worried about Jake or Christopher or even Lucas finding out about the operation. The plain truth was that they weren't sharp enough to notice changes in his behavior. But Zoey and Claire were different. They had advantages: Zoey because she was his sister, and Claire because in spite of their breakup, she still knew him—parts of him, anyway—better than anyone else.

Still, he'd put on a good act that morning on the ferry. He'd been all smiles. He'd also had a lucky break, what with Claire and Zoey spending the entire ride up on the deck—which had been very strange, come to think of it. The two of them *never* spent any time alone together if other people were around.

Just at that moment he became aware of someone standing in front of him, and he detected two distinct odors: coconut shampoo and dry tobacco. A smile broke out on his face. Nina. There was no mistaking her for anyone else in the world.

"Well, are you just going to stand there grinning like a jerk, or are you going to kiss me hello?"

"Oh, it's you." He titled his head, pretending to be surprised. "For a second I thought you were my *other* girlfriend."

"Gee, Benjamin, you're funny." She pecked him on the cheek, then slipped her arm under his and gently led him away from the school door. The voices of the other students began to fade. "Have you ever thought of a career in stand-up comedy?"

"Sure. The only thing holding me back is a fear of falling off the stage."

Nina laughed, then suddenly stopped.

Benjamin knew the reason. Usually she would have shot a joke right back, but that day any of his jokes would remind her of what she'd learned the previous night. With surgery possibly looming in the future, blindness was now a loaded subject. It would be better not to think about it at all.

"So where are we headed?" he asked softly, placing his hands over hers.

"I was thinking McDonald's," Nina said.

"Aha." Benjamin nodded. "A clean, well-lighted place."

"Hmmm. That sounds familiar."

"Very good, Nina," he said dryly. "It happens to

be the name of the short story you read to me a few weeks ago. Ernest Hemingway? Ring any bells?''

''Hey, you should've learned by now that when I read to you, I'm on autopilot.'' Her voice grew husky. ''My mouth and eyes are doing one thing, but my thoughts are somewhere else.''

Benjamin felt his face get hot. ''Mine, too, actually.'' He cleared his throat. ''Really, Nina—why are we going to McDonald's?''

''So we can have some privacy,'' Nina replied.

''Oh, right. Privacy.'' He drew in his breath. ''Uh . . . I hate to tell you this, but half the school goes there right about now.''

''Exactly,'' she said brightly. ''It'll be so noisy that nobody will notice us or hear a word we're saying. Anyway, I didn't feel like taking the ferry back with everyone else.''

Benjamin smiled. ''Brilliant, my dear Watson.''

''I figure the only thing we have to worry about is losing control and making out in front of hundreds of people.''

''We wouldn't want *that* to happen.''

''Nosiree. Public displays of affection are totally disgusting—especially in a fast-food joint.''

''Is Eesh meeting us there?''

''No.'' Nina chuckled. ''She's taking the water taxi back.''

''Twice in one day? Wow. Did the Grays just win the lottery or something?''

''She's worried about Christopher. Actually, *worried* is an understatement. She wasn't able to reach him on the phone last night, and since he thinks you two were 'doing the nasty'—to quote the sensitive words of Lucas Cabral—she figured she'd better hurry back and put his mind at ease. Before he does something crazy, as you males so often do."

Benjamin hesitated. "She's not going to tell—"

"Don't worry." Nina rubbed his arm soothingly. "She's going to use the same line you tried to use on me: that you two were working on a project."

"Well, we wouldn't want to stray too far from the truth." He sighed. "I guess it's a good thing she's telling him *something*. Although I doubt he's as crazy as you are."

"And what exactly do you mean by that?" she asked, feigning indignance.

"He's a pretty big guy." Benjamin shrugged. "I don't know if I could defend myself if he flew into a jealous rage. You saw how I did against Lara's boyfriend. Of course, he didn't know I was blind—" He broke off.

Nina didn't respond.

For an instant Benjamin felt bad. His humor was as much an instinct as his ability to concentrate, and for the same reason: self-preservation.

They walked for a while in silence. He sniffed the air and listened to the sounds of Weymouth: the chattering voices of students hurrying to get someplace warm, the purring motors of cars gliding slowly past—and just barely, in the distance, the steady rhythm of the tide lapping against the docks of Portside.

What would it be like to see all of that?

He'd never allowed himself to imagine what it would be like. He had memories of Weymouth from his childhood, but those memories had dimmed with time, in the same way that the faces of Nina and Zoey and his parents were just shadowy images out of the past, the faces of people who had grown and aged and changed. Soon after he'd lost his vision, he'd learned to keep a tight lid on his memory and imagination, because that path led to self-pity and depression and helplessness. Until now, he couldn't afford to dream.

He suddenly stopped short. "Nina—I have to tell you something."

Again there was no reply.

He forced himself to forge ahead. "I . . . uh, I've made a decision." He could hear the soft sound of her breath, faster than usual, communicating her grave, nervous anticipation. "I—I've decided to go to Boston this weekend," he stammered. His voice sounded strange and high-pitched to his own ears. Until he'd actually said the words, he still hadn't been certain he was really going to go through with it. "I mean, what's to lose?" he added quickly. "I'll just go have the tests done. . . ."

Before he knew it, Nina had taken him in her arms. Her body was trembling. He could feel her cheek, soft and warm and wet, against his. "I'm going with you," she whispered.

Benjamin realized with mild surprise that he was on the verge of crying, too. What was his problem, anyway? He was Benjamin Passmore, Mr. Confidence, the Blind Wonder. He was too strong for a stupid, melodramatic display over some lousy medical tests.

"I love you," he managed after a while.

"I know." Nina stood away from him, gripping his arms. She took a deep breath. "Listen. You need to tell your family."

"No." Benjamin shook his head. "I . . . can't. Not right now. I'm just gonna go check everything out. If things look good, then—"

"Benjamin, you *have* to tell them," she interrupted firmly. "Now that you've made a decision, they have a right to know."

"I understand where you're coming from. Believe me. But I have to do this my own way. There's—"

"What about Zoey?" Nina cried. "I mean—"

"Just let me finish. Mom and Dad have too much on their minds right now. With Lara around, it's not the easiest time at the old Passmore house, you know? And they can't afford to take any time off from the restaurant. I can't let them worry. If Zoey knows, she's going to tell them." He took a deep breath and drew her close again. "But I can't do this alone. That's why I need you there with me."

Nina didn't say anything for a long time.

"Can I count on you?" he whispered.

"Of course you can," she answered, sounding miserable. "Why do I always agree to everything you say?"

"Poor judgment?" he asked with a smile.

She laughed once. "So what are you proposing, exactly? That tomorrow after school we just hop on a bus to Boston? We just run away for the weekend? Just like that?"

"Well, we come up with a good excuse first . . . but in a nutshell, yes. That's exactly what I'm proposing."

Two thoughts consumed Aisha Gray as she sprinted down Leeward Drive toward Christopher Shupe's apartment. One was that Christopher was on the verge of doing something he would seriously regret. The other was that in less than seven hours, she'd managed to spend almost eighty dollars getting to and from Weymouth.

Objectively, problem number two wasn't exactly a big deal compared to problem number one. Nevertheless, with December twenty-fifth fast approaching, this wasn't the best time of year to be joyriding on the water taxi—especially given her mom's annoying insistence that the Gray family make a ridiculously big deal out of Christmas every year. Aisha had already done some of her shopping, but that day's pricey little round trip meant that at best, she'd have enough money left over for a couple of very low-budget cards.

Not that Christmas would really matter too much if Christopher put Benjamin in the hospital. Or worse.

Maybe I'm just overreacting, she thought for the thousandth time. *Christopher would never hurt Benjamin. . . .*

When Nina had told her at lunch about Christopher's late-night phone call to Lucas, Aisha had immediately flown into a panic. The last time Christopher had confided in Lucas, he'd ended up buying a gun to settle a score with some idiot skinheads who'd beaten him up. At the last moment he'd stopped himself from shooting, but he'd come close. Dangerously close.

Her lungs burning, Aisha took the steps of the old Victorian mansion two at a time. She dashed up the stairs to Christopher's room. The door was closed—and locked.

"Hello!" she cried breathlessly, banging on the door. "Christopher?"

After a few seconds, Christopher's soft, groggy voice answered. "Eesh?"

"It's me. Please let me in. . . ."

The door slowly creaked open.

Aisha immediately blushed.

The shades were drawn, and Christopher was wearing only boxers. He'd obviously been asleep. It wasn't that surprising, considering that he had to wake up at four-thirty for a paper route and work late at the Passmores' restaurant. But he certainly didn't look as if he'd been planning the crime of the century.

"What's up?" he asked confusedly. "Did you miss school today or something?"

In spite of her growing embarrassment, Aisha couldn't help but notice how good Christopher looked when he wore so little. "I—uh, thought I'd better come talk to you," she managed, struggling to catch her breath. "So, um, I took the water taxi home."

"This wouldn't happen to be about Benjamin, would it?" he asked.

"Christopher, it's not what you think—"

"I know it isn't."

She frowned. "You do?"

"Yeah." He was beginning to smile now. "Did you take the water taxi home just to tell me that?"

"Um, well," she began, feeling more foolish by the second, "I was just worried, you know, after that whole thing with the gun and everything . . . and when I tried to call you last night . . . I mean, it sounds stupid, but . . ."

"Come here," he whispered, drawing her into his arms. "Eesh, we trust each other."

"But I thought—"

"I'll admit I had my suspicions." He laughed. "Especially after the Jeff Pullings incident."

Aisha winced. "I can understand that," she said softly.

The two of them sat down on his bed. Christopher took her hand. "When I called Lucas last night, he made me realize how stupid I was being," he said. "He knows Benjamin would never cheat on Nina. And that got me thinking about you and me. I knew there had to be an explanation."

Aisha shook her head. "But Nina thought—"

"Nina's crazy, Eesh."

She had to laugh. "I guess you're right about that."

"When she told me some of the stuff you were saying, like 'You're really turning me on,' I knew that wasn't you." He grinned. "You don't talk like that."

"But it *was* me."

Christopher's grin instantly vanished.

"I mean, I was *reading* to him," she explained. "Off his computer screen."

He raised his eyebrows.

"Benjamin needed help surfing the Internet. I'm probably the only person on this island—besides Claire, maybe—who knows how to do it." She shrugged. "He needed a geek. Naturally he came to me."

"So much for African-American stereotypes," Christopher muttered. "So you were helping Benjamin look for some kind of online sex chat? Maybe *I* should learn more about the information superhighway."

Aisha slapped his arm playfully. "No, no, he was looking into this thing at Boston General Hospital—" She stopped.

Christopher's eyes widened. "The hospital? Why?"

Aisha felt sick. She couldn't believe she'd let that slip out. Actually, she could. It wasn't the first stupid mistake she'd made that day—not by a long shot.

"Is he sick or something?" Christopher asked worriedly.

"No, it's not that." Aisha sighed. She looked into his eyes. "Christopher, can you keep a secret? I mean, really keep a secret?"

Christopher leaned toward her so that their faces were only inches apart. "Babe, any secret you tell me is ours and ours alone."

"I'm serious, Christopher," she said, trying hard to sound convincing in spite of the way he was looking at her.

"So am I."

She took a deep breath. "Benjamin may be getting an operation that could restore his sight."

He blinked several times. "Whoa. That's . . . I don't know what that is. It's amazing."

"You have to swear you won't tell anyone."

"Of course I won't. But why doesn't he want to tell anyone? This is great news, isn't it?"

"He doesn't want to get anyone's hopes up in case it doesn't work out."

Christopher nodded thoughtfully. "I can understand that."

Aisha shook her head again. "I promised him I wouldn't tell anyone. . . ."

"Don't worry about it." He leaned forward and kissed her, running his hands through her long, thick brown curls. In spite of her worry, she couldn't help but feel an electric tingle of excitement.

"You need to take your mind off Benjamin," he whispered.

She closed her eyes and nodded. She'd made a fool out of herself one too many times that day. "You're right," she breathed. "And I think I know the perfect distraction."

Four

Zoey had never been so glad to get off the ferry. She was exhausted—but at least she'd decided on a course of action. After spending all of history class and French class and the entire ferry ride home with Lucas, she knew what she had to do. She had to march right up Climbing Way and tell Aaron that their kiss had been an accident, a fluke—a terrible mistake that could never happen again.

She was in love. Totally, absolutely, head over heels in love. And *not* with Aaron Mendel. Sure, he was drop-dead gorgeous. He was also sensitive and talented—but so what? He *wasn't* Lucas.

Zoey squeezed Lucas's hand, reassured by his presence. As the two of them walked across the parking lot at the ferry landing, her eyes wandered in the fading sunlight over the roof of her parents' restaurant to the Grays' B&B perched above North Harbor. All she had to do was go up there and end it. Right away.

And then I can put the whole thing behind me. It'll be just like it never happened.

". . . sure you're okay?"

"Huh?" She jumped slightly and turned toward Lucas. She hadn't even realized he'd been talking.

31

"Yeah, yeah," she said quickly. "I'm sorry. It's just that I didn't sleep. You know, Lara's—"

"Been driving you crazy," he finished, anticipating her words. His voice was flat and exasperated. "I know. You told me four times already."

Zoey stopped walking when they reached the corner of Bristol Street. She forced a smile, but Lucas's brown eyes remained blank under the rim of his black wool cap. He took his hand from hers and brushed a few strands of blond hair out of his face.

"Look, Lucas, I'm sorry," she said quietly. She stared down at the cobblestones, unable to bring herself to look at him directly. "I know I haven't been myself lately. It's just that . . . I've got a lot on my mind."

"I *know*, Zoey." He put a gloved hand under her chin and gently lifted her head until their gazes locked. "That's why I'm worried about you. I want you to tell me what's bothering you." His eyes hardened. "What's *really* bothering you."

Zoey blinked. Suddenly she felt very hot, even though the freezing ocean wind had numbed her ears and the tip of her nose. Her heart was racing. Had she been acting *that* strange? Maybe she had. Even Claire had noticed she'd been distracted on the ferry that morning.

"I told you what's bothering me," she said, just to fill the silence. "Lara."

Lucas let his hand drop. He laughed once and shook his head. "I give up. I can't force it out of you. But when two people are . . ." He hesitated. "When two people are in a relationship, they're supposed to share things. They're supposed to help each other out. Right?"

Zoey held her breath. He'd been going to say "when two people are in love," but he'd stopped himself. There was no use trying to maintain the lie— to convince Lucas that Lara's presence in her house was the sole source of her misery. It wasn't working. Lucas knew her far too well.

"Look, Lucas," she said finally. "I—I can't tell you what's bothering me." Her voice was barely a whisper. "Not right now, anyway."

Lucas nodded, his jaw tightly set. "Well, when you decide, give me a call, all right? Until then, I guess you're on your own." He turned and began walking down Bristol Street.

"Lucas," she called after him. "Please . . ." But it was too late. He disappeared around the corner.

Zoey hung her head. She was a lousy liar, and she knew it. The problem was that everyone else knew it, too. Most likely Lucas hadn't bought her lame story about having to meet Aisha just then, either. Why was it that she had to pepper every falsehood with a half-truth? *Something* was bothering her, but she couldn't say what. She *had* been at the Grays' house the previous night, but not looking for Eesh. Why couldn't she just be like everyone else and BS convincingly for once in her life?

A thought occurred to her quite suddenly: *I didn't want to hurt Lucas, but I already have.*

Zoey began the slow, scenic hike up Climbing Way. The sun had long since fallen below the horizon. The lights of Weymouth twinkled brightly on the other side of the bay, and directly below her were the quaint houses of North Harbor. In a way, the night was comforting. It represented closure. She'd had her one official day of two-timing, and it had been a complete failure. Now the day was over. She would say good-bye to Aaron and fall back into the warm, familiar arms of Lucas.

But what if Lucas demanded an explanation?

Stop it! she commanded herself. So what if he did? He deserved an explanation. Of course, she would have to lie again, but this time she'd do a good job. . . .

Squinting up the hill, she could see that the light was on in the second-floor guest room Aaron occupied. Good. She could even see his silhouette through the curtains. He was sitting on the edge of his bed, hunched over something. He was playing his guitar. Yes, she could see him strumming, moving his head back and forth in time to the music she couldn't hear. She could almost imagine his voice . . .

Zoey felt short of breath. She shook her head. It was just the cold and the steepness of the climb; that was all. It *wasn't* Aaron Mendel.

She marched across the lawn, picked up a pebble, and threw it at Aaron's window.

The shadow in the room froze, then put down the guitar and parted the curtain.

Zoey swallowed.

There was no denying it—Aaron was beautiful. Everything about him was beautiful: his olive skin, his chiseled bones, his piercing hazel eyes. Even when he was squinting through the glass, he was undeniably devastating.

A bright smile broke on his face. He quickly shoved the window open.

"Hey, what's up?" He wrinkled his nose at the sight of his own frozen exhalation. "Wow. It's cold. Come on in before you freeze to death."

Zoey shook her head. "Aaron, I . . ." She couldn't say it.

"Zoey, come in," he said imploringly.

What the hell is your problem? she silently screamed at herself. *Say what you have to say and get out!* But for some reason her mouth had suddenly become incapable of producing any sound.

"Look, I know why you're here." His smile had changed. It was sympathetic now—in a strange, almost sad way. "Just come in so we can talk."

Zoey nodded mutely.

Aaron met her at the front door and led her quickly up the stairs to his room. In spite of all the self-loathing and embarrassment, Zoey once again felt that curious thrill she had felt the night before: the thrill of sneaking around behind her friends' backs. She was in Aisha's house, but none of the Grays knew it. She was there in that quaint little room, with its four-poster bed, polished wood floor, and thick rugs, and nobody but Aaron knew where she was.

"Look, Zoey," he said, sitting on the edge of the bed, "I'm sorry about what happened last night."

The comment caught her off guard. "Sorry?" she repeated. She shifted nervously on her feet. "Why?"

He picked up his guitar and began strumming absently. "Because I know you have a boyfriend." He stared at the curtains. "I feel like . . . I feel like I forced you into a situation you didn't want to be in."

"Nobody forced anything," she found herself saying. "*I* came to see you, remember?"

He turned to look at her, then looked away again. "What I'm trying to say is . . . I'll understand if you want to avoid me. You know, until I leave."

"Avoid you?" Zoey swallowed. She inched forward slightly, unable to tear her eyes from him. "I don't want to avoid you, Aaron," she whispered.

His head turned slowly until their eyes met. "You don't?" he asked.

She shook her head.

"Then why did you come here?"

Zoey paused. Why *had* she come here? Her thoughts had become very hazy. She'd spent all day coming up with a logical, perfectly rational explanation for why she wanted to come here, why she *had* to come here—but at that moment her mind was a blank. "I guess I don't know," she murmured.

"I think I do," he said gently. His hazel eyes glittered in the soft light of the room. "I think it's because you're a very loyal girlfriend, and you realize that what you did last night was an impulsive mistake." He smiled. "Am I right?"

"I don't think you are."

The words popped out of her mouth almost before she knew she was saying them. *Stupid!* Why couldn't she control herself? Why was she thinking one thing and doing another? She furiously struggled to summon an image of Lucas in her mind's eye, to conjure up his face—but all she could manage was a confused mishmash of Jake and Lucas somehow mixed together. It was all wrong; she couldn't be thinking of Lucas in the same way she thought of Jake—as an ex-boyfriend. Lucas *was* the reason she was there, wasn't he?

"I think you'd better go," Aaron said.

Zoey nodded, but she was frozen. She was unable to do anything but watch. She watched as Aaron put his guitar down. She watched as he stood up. She watched as he walked over to her and put his hands on her arms.

"I think you'd better go," he repeated thickly.

Zoey nodded again. Only this time she closed her eyes and let her mouth melt in a soft kiss against Aaron's lips.

LUCAS

I don't have any deep, dark secrets. It may sound hard to believe, but it's true. Everything in my life is pretty much out in the open. I spent two years in Youth Authority for killing Wade McRoyan, even though I didn't do it. I don't get along with my father. I'm in love with Zoey Passmore and I really want to have sex with her. I also cheated on her. The general public is aware of all these important facts.

I really think it's much better that way. To be honest, I hate secrets. Secrets suck. I should know. I used to have a lot of them, and they almost destroyed my life on several occasions. Now, for the first time since I was about three, I can truly say that I have nothing to hide. And I feel damn good about it.

The biggest problem I have is

that for some strange reason people want to tell me _their_ secrets. Like when Christopher told me he wanted a gun. Or people don't want to tell me their secrets, but I find out anyway. So a lot of my deepest, darkest secrets aren't even mine—they're somebody else's. As you may have already guessed, this is a lousy predicament for somebody who doesn't like secrets to begin with.

If I had it my way, there wouldn't be any such thing as a deep, dark secret. Everybody would just say exactly what was on his or her mind.

Or they would shut up.

But it's not a perfect world, is it?

Five

The air was much too cold for Lucas to be pacing around on the deck, but he couldn't stop. He'd been out there for almost two hours. His face and hands were in serious pain. Of course, right at that moment, pain wasn't necessarily a bad thing. Some good old-fashioned pain would remind him of what a jerk he'd just been.

Once again he'd managed to royally screw up things with Zoey. A pretty clear pattern was forming: When life was going well, Lucas Cabral could be counted on to hop right in and ruin it. He just had a knack for failure. The mistakes kept coming. He'd even started a mental list:

LUCAS CABRAL'S LIFE-SHATTERING MISTAKES
(IN NO PARTICULAR ORDER)

Mistake number one: falling in love with Claire. (Because of misguided loyalty to her, he'd spent two years locked away with the lowest forms of human life, such as the skinheads who'd beaten up Christopher.)

Mistake number two: cheating on Zoey. (He'd fooled

around with Claire because he'd thought Zoey was trying to get back together with Jake.)

Mistake number three (more than once): Pressuring Zoey to sleep with him. (His incessant demands that they hop in the sack only made him look like the sex-crazed lunatic he was.)

Mistake number four (more than once): being in the wrong place at the wrong time. (The car crash that had killed Jake's brother was the best example, although there were about four million others.)

Mistake number five (more than once): losing his temper. (He'd ruined the Geigers' party the previous Friday night because Zoey happened to talk to another male . . .)

It was pointless to continue, he realized, because he'd be out there all night. He glanced down at the Passmore house. No lights were on. Zoey wouldn't be home for a while; she'd said something about having to talk to Aisha. Knowing the two of them, Zoey probably wouldn't get home until eight at the earliest. Why was it that girls loved to chat so much? Conversations between guys were much simpler: They exchanged vital information. Guys never just "chatted."

Then again, Lucas could talk to Zoey about anything. So why couldn't she tell him what was bothering her? Maybe because she was bothered about some other guy. That guy Aaron, maybe? Or what if she wanted to get back together with Jake? After all, Jake and Claire weren't going out anymore. Jake was up for grabs.

Anger began to swell within Lucas once more—followed quickly by remorse, then by self-pity. He shook his head. There was no way Zoey wanted to get back together with Jake. Lucas had been going through this same cycle of emotions all day. It was wearing him out. He needed to do something about this, right away.

In the blackness of the water beyond the Passmore house, Lucas noticed a mass of lights gliding slowly away from the island. The 6:55 ferry was just pulling out. An idea dawned on him: This would be the perfect time to pay the Passmores a visit. He knew Benjamin had been on that ferry. Lucas could just pop by, looking for Zoey. Benjamin, of course, would let him in. And during that time, Lucas and Benjamin would do some chatting.

Zoey doesn't get involved with my relationships, and I don't get involved with hers, Benjamin had told him that morning. Of course not. But he and Benjamin never really talked that much anymore—just the two of them, man to man, that is. It would be good to hang out. And since Lucas was Zoey's boyfriend, and Benjamin was Zoey's brother . . . well, it wasn't inconceivable that her name would come up. A casual question about Zoey wouldn't seem too out of the blue, would it?

Another blast of wind whipped at Lucas's face. Without hesitating, he hopped over the deck railing, twisted, and lowered himself until he was suspended above the Passmores' lawn. Then he dropped. After rolling across the frozen earth, he hopped up, dusted himself off, and walked around to the front of Zoey's house.

Perfect timing. Benjamin and Nina were just walking across the gravel toward the front walk. Now if only he could figure out a way to get rid of Nina . . .

Benjamin froze. "Nina, quick—get the shotgun!" he cried. "Somebody's sneaking around our house! Blow his head off!"

"Very humorous." Lucas made a face. "You're lucky it's me."

"No, you're lucky I have psychic powers, Lucas," he said sarcastically. "That's how I can tell you apart from the hundreds of others who jump off *your* back porch into *our* backyard."

"Do I still have permission to blow his head off?" Nina asked eagerly.

"Oh, I think we can let him live," Benjamin said, pushing the door open into pitch blackness. "Zoey might start wondering why her boyfriend suddenly disappeared."

Nina turned on the front hall light. "Hello!" she called. "Anyone home?"

"Hi," came a faint voice from somewhere upstairs.

"Hi, Lara," Benjamin called, obviously making an effort to sound enthusiastic.

"Does she have an aversion to lights or something?" Lucas whispered. He rubbed the sides of his arms in an effort to warm himself.

"Your guess is as good as mine," Benjamin said under his breath. He turned and fixed his dark glasses in the direction of Lucas's eyes, demonstrating his uncanny ability to simulate eye contact. "Well, I guess Zoey isn't home yet."

"Oh. Hey, is it cool if I just hang out and wait for her?" Lucas asked, trying not to sound too hopeful.

Benjamin hesitated for a second. Did he want to be

alone with Nina just then? Nina was staring at him, poised for a response.

"Uh—sure," he said finally. "No problem."

Nina rolled her eyes. "Well, now that any romantic possibilities have been spoiled, I think I'll just go on home." She kissed Benjamin on the cheek and opened the door again, but not before leering at Lucas. "Thanks a lot."

"My pleasure," Lucas said sincerely.

Benjamin smiled. "Call me later, all right?"

"Don't worry. You'll be hearing from me." Nina closed the door behind her.

"You hungry at all?" Benjamin asked, hanging up his coat in the front hall closet. He headed for the kitchen. "I'm starved, myself."

"Sure," Lucas said, following him. He slouched at the table while Benjamin rummaged through the refrigerator. Watching Benjamin in his own home was actually a pretty incredible sight. Except for the dark glasses and the way he ran his fingers lightly over most of the items, there was no way to tell that Benjamin was blind.

Benjamin's hand stopped at a microwave container on one of the lower shelves. "Leftover pasta," he announced. "That sound okay to you?"

"Fine by me."

Benjamin popped the container into the microwave and sat across from him. For a moment there was silence between them. "Well, well, well," Benjamin finally said with a crafty smile. "So why do I get the feeling you knew Zoey wasn't gonna be here?"

"I—I didn't . . . ," Lucas stammered, then stopped himself. He had to laugh.

Benjamin continued to smile back, as if to say, *You*

should know better than to try to pull something over on me, Cabral.

"You want to know what's bothering Zoey, don't you?" he asked.

There was no point in trying to lie at this point. "Of course I do," Lucas said.

"You know the Passmore rule, Lucas."

He sighed. "Yeah, yeah," he mumbled, sounding more dejected than he would have liked.

"Well, the fact of the matter is that I have no idea what's bothering Zoey. I'm kind of curious myself."

Lucas leaned back in his chair and studied Benjamin's face. He looked as if he were telling the truth, but then again, Benjamin was pretty good at concealing his emotions. If Zoey were seeing or even thinking about seeing somebody else, would she tell her big brother? Probably not. It wouldn't hurt to ask, though. . . .

"You don't believe me?" Benjamin asked.

"No, I believe you," Lucas said resignedly. "I was just wondering if you—"

The piercing beep of the microwave timer cut him off, followed immediately by the sound of the doorbell ringing.

"Good Lord." Benjamin hopped up. "Sounds like the end of the world. Hey, grab some plates, will you?" He walked into the front hall and unlocked the door.

"Hey, Benjamin."

Lucas froze. It was Jake.

"Dad!" Benjamin exclaimed. "How's it going?"

"You've been spending way too much time with Nina, man," Jake said. "Your sense of humor has taken a serious turn for the worse."

45

"I'll take that as a compliment."

White-hot anger flashed through Lucas. There was only one possible explanation for why Jake had come here: to see Zoey. And that meant Lucas would have to beat the crap out of him. Plain and simple.

"You guys eating?" Jake asked calmly.

"Lucas and I were just sitting down to some spaghetti," Benjamin replied. "Zoey isn't here. But you're welcome to join us."

Yeah, just come on in here, man, Lucas thought. *Come on in and join me.*

"Uh . . . no, thanks." Jake cleared his throat. He sounded uncomfortable. "I was actually wondering if Lara was around."

"Lara?" Lucas blurted. What kind of lame excuse was that? Unable to control himself, he marched into the front hall. "You're here to see *Lara*? Nice try."

Jake was standing there with his hands in his coat pockets. He didn't look angry, just mildly surprised. "Yeah. As a matter of fact I am. Why do you care?"

"I don't," Lucas spat.

"Fine. So what's your problem?"

"My problem is that you're lying."

"Look, man, I don't know what you're on right now, but I am *not* here to see Zoey. And even if I were, it wouldn't be any of *your* damn business."

"That's where you're wrong." He took a step toward Jake. "I'd make it my busi—"

"Lucas, *shut the hell up!*" Benjamin barked.

Everyone froze.

Lucas's eyes widened.

Never in his entire life had he seen Benjamin explode like that. Ever.

"You two morons are not going to fight in my

house,'' Benjamin stated in a cold, dead voice. He jerked a shaky finger toward the door. "Lara's in her room. You have to take the stairs by the garage. If you want to see her, be my guest.''

Jake glanced slack-jawed at Lucas. Without another word, he turned and hurried out the door, slamming it behind him.

"Why did he even bother coming in here?'' Benjamin brushed past Lucas, heading back toward the kitchen. "Let's eat.''

Lucas bit his lip. "Hey, Benjamin, I'm really sorry about that, all right?'' he said tentatively. "I didn't mean—''

"Forget it.'' Benjamin sat at the table and put his head in his hands. For a moment he sat perfectly still, breathing deeply. Then he sat up straight. He looked very pale.

Lucas couldn't move. What had just happened? In the blink of an eye, the situation in the Passmore house had become not only extremely weird, but scary. Benjamin Passmore was the model of coolness; nothing ever fazed him. Not unless something was terribly, terribly wrong.

"Are you okay?'' he asked.

"Of course I am, Lucas,'' Benjamin said derisively. "Why do you ask?''

Lucas didn't say anything. He couldn't think of anything *to* say. He just wanted to get out of that house as fast as possible.

"Lucas, I know why you came down here. And I'm sorry to say I don't have any information about your girlfriend. So whaddaya say we enjoy our spaghetti in silence, all right?''

47

"Uh . . . I think I lost my appetite," Lucas said, very aware of how foolish he sounded.

Benjamin flashed a brief, humorless smile. "I kinda figured you would."

Nina

My deepest, darkest secret? I really shouldn't tell. Well, okay. I'm actually an alien from the planet Zorf, sent here to destroy all of mankind, starting with Savage Garden. I have assumed the form of a devastatingly attractive, brilliantly witty sixteen-year-old girl until I decide the moment is right to unleash my fury upon the poor, ignorant people of Earth. . . .

Hey, seriously. To be honest, my deepest, darkest secret doesn't have to do with me at all. Nope. It's about my sister, Claire.

You see, she's been worshipping Satan for quite a few years now, and recently she and the Prince of Darkness have moved beyond the casual-friends stage. It's only a matter of time before someone sees the two of them making out up there on her widow's walk during a blizzard or freak lightning storm.

Still not good enough?

Hmmm. The problem is... I guess I'd have to say that secrets — especially deep, dark ones — aren't exactly my favorite topic of conversation. In fact, I'd rank deep, dark secrets (my own, that is) right up there with what _really_ goes into the menu at the Weymouth High School cafeteria.

It doesn't take a budding
Einstein to figure out why.

For a long time I had a secret
that I kept hidden — a secret
that still hurts when I think
about it. And it still causes me
nightmares, although I have those
less and less. It was about what
my uncle did to me when I stayed
at his house.

It was a secret that caused me
a lot of terror and shame.

But when I decided to tell
everyone the truth, the terror
and the shame started to go
away. And pretty soon after
that, Benjamin became my boyfriend.
Life is good, as they say in beer
commercials.

So naturally I'm not a real big fan of keeping deep, dark secrets. I guess I do have one, though. The stupid thing is, it's a secret about something that hasn't even happened yet. And it might not ever happen.

It's a secret about how scared I am. How scared of something that <u>could</u> happen.

And what exactly could Nina Geiger possibly be so scared of?

Well, here it is: The operation is a success. Benjamin gets the bandages taken off his eyes, and all of us are crowding around his bed. He blinks a few times and looks around the room. Then he sees

Claire. He yells, "Nina! You're more beautiful then I ever imagined!" and leaps into her arms. Then there's about forty-five minutes of awkward silence until somebody — Mrs. Passmore, probably — gets up the nerve to tell him that no, that's not Nina, that's Claire. Nina is over <u>there</u>.

Then Benjamin looks at me.

Then he hurls.

Some secret, huh?

Six

After nudging up the volume on her stereo one more time, Nina turned back in frustration to the half-filled suitcase on her bed. The floor was now vibrating under the onslaught of Green Day's guitar crunch. It was a good thing nobody was home. Neither her dad nor Claire was sympathetic to the fact that deafening music helped her concentrate.

She'd been pacing back and forth between her closet and her bed for the past half hour, taking one article of clothing after another and throwing them in her suitcase—only to snatch them back out again and toss them onto the floor.

Why did she even care so much? It wasn't as though Benjamin would be able to see what she was wearing. She could dress up like Bugs Bunny for all he knew.

She walked over to the closet one last time and grabbed a pair of torn green fatigues that she knew Zoey, Aisha, and Claire hated. Yes, that was the nice thing about having a blind boyfriend—Nina could make any fashion statement she wanted. In fact, she could put on four hundred pounds and he wouldn't be able to tell. Well, that wasn't quite true; he'd have a hard time giving her a hug. She could become a leper, though, or lose her nose. . . .

But what if Benjamin could see?

Suddenly she thought back to the three jelly doughnuts she'd eaten for breakfast that morning. She looked down at her stubby, ragged-looking fingernails. She glanced in the mirror at her long, dark, unkempt hair and makeupless face.

She felt queasy, and it wasn't just the doughnuts. Benjamin would open his eyes that fateful day and see a poorly groomed heifer. *Okay*, she resolved, *no more doughnuts*. No more Doritos and no more Ben and Jerry's. She'd stop chewing on her fingernails. She'd get a haircut. She'd finally give in to the makeover Zoey was always threatening her with.

"Damn it, Nina!"

Uh-oh. Nina whipped around to see Claire storming across the room. She pushed past Nina and with a violent twist turned the volume all the way down to zero.

"Sorry," Nina mumbled, still clutching the pair of pants. "I didn't think anyone was home."

"I just walked in," Claire said crossly. "Nina, what are you thinking? I could hear this all the way from—" Her tirade abruptly stopped when she saw the suitcase. "What are you doing?" she demanded.

Nina folded the fatigues and tossed them on the bed, careful not to meet Claire's gaze. "Benjamin got tickets to the Boston Philharmonic, and he wants me to go with him," she said quickly. "It was kind of a last-minute thing—I mean, he just told me today, but I thought it would be fun to get off the island for the weekend." She turned back to the closet and grabbed a sweatshirt. "You know, especially considering that the last road trip to Boston was a total failure. I mean, we never even made it to Massachusetts.''

''Does Dad know about this?''

Nina glanced at her sister. Claire was standing in the doorway with her arms folded across her chest, but she no longer looked mad. Only curious.

''Well, uh—no,'' Nina said. She swallowed. ''He's out with Sarah right now. He left a note. He's not going to be home until late. I'll tell him tomorrow at breakfast.''

''You don't think he'll have a problem with it?''

''Why would he?'' Nina turned back to the stereo and increased the volume again, making sure that the music was only barely audible. ''He loves Benjamin. You know that.''

''Yes, I do,'' Claire replied.

Nina looked at her again. For some reason Claire wasn't moving. Usually she couldn't stand to be in Nina's room. But now she was just standing there staring at Nina, with the faint beginnings of a smirk forming on her lips.

Nina pretended to busy herself with packing— grabbing mismatched socks and hurling them into the suitcase—but after about ten seconds she lost control. ''Don't you have something to do?'' she barked. ''Like howl at the moon or cast spells or fly around on your broomstick?''

''Actually, I thought we could spend some quality time together,'' Claire replied with mock earnestness. She sat down next to the suitcase on Nina's bed. ''Now that Dad's gone so much of the time with Sarah, I think it's important that we sisters stick together. You know, to maintain family ties.''

''I'm touched, Claire,'' Nina whispered through

tightly clenched teeth. Why was Claire doing this? She was sitting very calmly with her long dark hair cascading over her shoulders and her flawless, ice-cold features set in an ironic grin. She'd been smiling far too much that day. Nina wanted to smack her.

"Look," Nina said finally. "I turned down the music. Please, just get out of here."

"Gladly. As soon as you tell me the *real* reason you're packing this suitcase. Believe me, I don't want to prolong the torture any more than you do."

"I told you the reason," Nina answered, knowing how unconvincing she sounded and hating herself for it.

Claire shook her head. "Nina, please don't try to lie to me. You know how useless it is. Lying is not your specialty."

"What makes you think I'm lying?"

"Well, for one, you're acting even more psychotic than usual," Claire remarked tonelessly. "Also, when you lie, you avoid people's eyes and talk too fast. And you lose your sense of humor—not that that's a bad thing."

Nina lowered her eyes. Claire was right. She was pathetically transparent. There was nothing she could do about it now; Claire wouldn't leave until she forced the truth out of her. That was the great thing about good old Claire: She always had to push and push and push until she got exactly what she wanted. Why couldn't she have an older sister like Zoey or Eesh . . . anybody except the Wicked Witch of Chatham Island?

"Well?" Claire prompted.

Nina took a deep breath, then flopped down on the bed on the other side of the suitcase. "Fine, Claire."

She leaned back and stared at the ceiling. "Only you have to swear to me that what I tell you never leaves this room."

"You're not in any kind of trouble, are you?" Claire asked, sounding genuinely concerned.

"No, no—nothing like that." Nina couldn't help but laugh. "I'm not pregnant or anything."

"I *know* you're not pregnant," Claire said, a little too emphatically. "I was thinking more along the lines of suspension."

Claire hadn't meant anything by the comment, but now an uncomfortable silence hung in the air. Was it really *that* far-fetched that she could have gotten pregnant? It was true that she and Benjamin had never slept together—but still, why was Claire so sure they hadn't? Was it because Claire thought that Benjamin still considered the younger Geiger sister to be nothing more than an amusing kid?

Another thought suddenly occurred to Nina: Claire *wasn't* a virgin. At least Nina was pretty sure she wasn't.

Benjamin hasn't slept with me—but he probably slept with Claire.

Nina's stomach turned. She had considered that possibility before, but never really seriously. Only now did it seem so painfully obvious.

"So what's up?" Claire asked, unable to mask her impatience.

Nina shook her head. She couldn't bear to think about that anymore. "Benjamin may have found an operation that can cure his blindness. He wants me to go with him to check it out."

"Ha, ha."

"I'm serious."

Claire sighed. "You're not being funny, Nina. You're being sick."

"You wanted the truth—and I'm giving it to you," Nina said tersely. She sat up straight and looked Claire in the eye. "Benjamin and Eesh were surfing the Internet last week, and they came across a bulletin board at Boston General. The hospital is looking for volunteers for some kind of experimental surgery that has a fifty percent chance of reversing blindness. Benjamin is going there this weekend to have some tests done to see if he's eligible or not. He wants me to go with him. *That's* the truth." Her voice rose a notch. "Satisfied?"

Claire blinked. "Oh, my God," she whispered.

"You've got that right," Nina said, collapsing back onto the bed.

"What does Zoey think about all this?" Claire asked after a minute.

"She doesn't know." Nina rubbed her eyes, feeling strangely exhausted. "Nobody knows except Eesh and me . . . and now you."

"Why on earth—"

"Benjamin doesn't want to get anyone's hopes up," Nina interrupted. "Look, it might not even work out. I mean, he's only going in for tests. He might not even be eligible. And even if he is, there's a very good possibility the operation—if and when it does happen—won't work."

"What does Benjamin think about all this?"

"He doesn't know what to think. I guess he's probably scared."

Claire was quiet for several seconds. "Benjamin is . . ." She didn't finish.

Nina shifted her position to get a look at Claire's

face. Her smile had vanished, and her eyes had taken on an odd, vacant glaze. Her expression seemed pained. For a moment Nina almost felt bad she'd been so harsh.

"Benjamin is what?" she asked.

"He's brave," Claire finally managed.

"I know."

Claire stood up, still looking somewhat uncertain. "I hope . . . I hope everything goes well."

"Look at it this way: he's got nothing to lose," Nina said. She tried hard to sound reassuring, as much for herself as for Claire.

Claire walked toward the door, then paused. "Nina, you know Benjamin sometimes has a hard time talking, I mean *really* talking, about the way he feels, and I—"

"He doesn't have that problem with me," Nina interrupted. Her goodwill faded. Claire *definitely* didn't need to give her advice on how to handle Benjamin—especially right at that moment. "Don't worry about it. I'll take care of him. You just make sure that Dad thinks I'm going to expand my horizons by going to hear some classical music."

Claire nodded. She opened her mouth as if she was about to say something, then closed it. For once in her life, Nina realized, Claire wasn't able to supply the final word.

"What's the matter, Jakie?" Lara murmured. "You look stressed."

Jake sat on the edge of Lara's bed, watching as she moved around the room and dimmed what few lights were on. As usual, he felt overly hot and anxious in her presence. She was dressed in a dark shirt and jeans, both of which were so tight that she looked as if her naked body had just been dipped in black ink. He was having a very hard time taking his eyes off her—not that she seemed to mind.

"You aren't having any regrets about last night, are you?" she whispered, sitting beside him. She grazed his thigh with long black fingernails.

Jake shook his head, twitching involuntarily every time her fingers inched up his jeans. The previous night, Lara had sneaked over to his house—and stayed until six A.M. They'd sworn to each other that neither of them was going to touch another drop of alcohol. After that, they hadn't done too much talking.

"I wouldn't be here if I did," he said finally.

"So what's up?"

"It's just that . . . Benjamin kinda flipped out just now. I've never really seen him like that." He ran a hand through his short, wiry brown hair. "He's usually a pretty calm and collected guy, you know?"

"He's very smart, isn't he?"

Jake nodded, thinking, *A lot smarter than I'll ever be*.

Lara's lips brushed his ear. "I know something about Benjamin."

He frowned. "You aren't gonna try to tell me that his father is a demon or anything, are you?"

"No, no," she said with a laugh. "I told you, all that stuff was a joke."

Jake just shrugged. The night he'd first met her, they'd gotten very drunk, and she'd done a lot of very weird things—not the least of which had been pretending to contact his dead brother with a Quija board. He'd even seen Wade just before passing out. But there was no point in getting into *that* again. "So what

61

do you know about Benjamin?'' he asked.

"He's looking into some sort of operation that will cure his blindness."

"What?"

"It's true. He wants to keep it a secret, though. He has no idea I know."

For a moment Jake managed to forget that her hand was on his leg. "How *do* you know?"

She smiled in a strange, secretive way, then stood up. "Come here," she said, taking his hand. She led him over to the side of the room that bordered on the rest of the house and gestured to a little grate in the floor. "That vent connects to the hall right outside Benjamin's bathroom," she said with a wink. "I can hear everything."

Jake pushed her hand aside in disgust. "Are you telling me that you listen in on Benjamin?"

"I don't *listen in*, Jakie," she growled. "But when he's having a really loud conversation or blasting opera or something, it's kind of hard not to hear."

Jake just shook his head.

"You're not gonna go all moral on me now, are you?" Lara said with a sneer.

"Go all moral on you? No, I would never think of doing that, Lara," Jake said sarcastically. "I know that wouldn't work with you."

"Hey, I—" Suddenly Lara's face softened. "Look, I'm sorry." She walked back to the bed. "All I heard was Benjamin talking to that girl Aisha. They were using his computer to look into some sort of operation. Let's just forget it."

"But I—"

"It's no big deal." She stretched out on the mattress and propped her head up with her right arm.

"Come back over here," she whispered, slapping the bed with her left hand.

Jake just stared at her. No big deal? Was that what she thought?

"Come on. We've done enough talking for one night, don't you think?"

We probably have. He couldn't decide whether to stay or to leave. Why was it that every time he hung out with Lara, something happened to make him think that getting involved with her was a huge mistake? He *could* just leave. He had a paper to write that night—something for English class on *The Scarlet Letter*, a book he still hadn't finished. Maybe he should just get started.

"Come on, Jakie," she breathed, scratching the blankets with her fingernails. "Come here."

Then again, maybe he could stay just a little while longer.

Seven

It was almost nine-thirty by the time Zoey got home. Luckily her parents were still at the restaurant. Lara was upstairs, doing who knew what. Soft blues was playing in Benjamin's room; Nina was probably in there with him, and most likely they didn't want to be disturbed. Zoey allowed herself a sigh of relief. She was safe from everyone's questions—at least for now.

"I woke up this morning, had them walkin' blues," the crackly voice sang behind Benjamin's closed door. *"I woke up this morning, had them walkin' blues. . . ."*

For a moment Zoey closed her eyes, letting the tinny sound of the guitar take her back to where she had just spent the last four hours. Aaron had played a few songs for her. He'd sung to her. And then he'd taken her in his arms again. . . .

She hurried up the stairs and flopped down on her bed. Her mind was a blur; one minute she felt giddy, and the next she was stricken with remorse. But she knew she couldn't procrastinate any longer. The next day she would have to tell Lucas how she felt about Aaron. It was only fair.

There's one problem.

I still love Lucas.

A woman could be in love with two people at the same time, though, couldn't she? It had happened before. Zoey had read hundreds—well, maybe not hundreds, but *dozens*—of books in which a troubled heroine was caught between the passions of two strong, gallant, honorable men. *Gallant* didn't quite describe Lucas, considering that practically every time he said hello, he suggested they sleep together. But he *was* strong and honorable. Aaron, of course, didn't even believe in premarital sex. So he was all of the above. Not to mention intelligent, funny, and more handsome than anyone she'd ever met. He was like some fairy-tale prince come to life.

Zoey laughed to herself, remembering the princes she'd described in the first chapter of the big romance novel she'd planned to write. She must have written those opening pages over twenty-five times. Most of the princes had been like Jake. Toward the end, they'd been like Lucas. And then when she'd learned about her parents' infidelities, she'd thrown the whole thing into the garbage.

She shook her head. Even her own *mother* had been in love with two men at once.

Was Zoey in the minority by thinking that infidelity was such a bad thing? Maybe people just had to learn to live with their imperfections. Her parents had certainly learned how. In fact, they were more in love now than ever before.

Aaron was leaving the island in less than a month; in all likelihood she wouldn't see him for another six months. And she'd see him again only if Mr. Geiger and Ms. Mendel were still an item. Did she really want to lose Lucas over a little fling? Maybe it would be best for everyone if he never found out. Or at least, if he didn't find out for another twenty years or so—like her dad.

Claire's words echoed through her mind: *Adultery is such an interesting topic, don't you think?*

Zoey had answered no a little too quickly.

Which reminded her of something. She still had to finish *The Scarlet Letter* and write a 1,750-word essay on it.

It looked as though it was going to be another long, sleepless night.

"I woke up this morning, had them walkin' blues . . ."

Benjamin stood in front of his closet, humming quietly along with Blind Lemon Jefferson. Packing was never his favorite activity, but at least he could do it on his own. His mom had helped him arrange his shirts and pants in such a way that he always knew exactly where everything was. Even if he somehow became confused, his wardrobe was predominantly black and white, so he was never in too much danger of wearing an absurd mismatch.

"I sold my soul, but I ain't got nothin' to lose . . ."

The last half of the line spoke the truth, Benjamin reminded himself. He and Nina had been telling each other the same thing over and over again that afternoon. He yanked a couple of shirts and pants from the hangers and, after deftly folding them, let them fall into the canvas bag he'd placed at his feet. No, he knew he had nothing to lose. It was the first half of the line that bothered him.

Selling one's soul wasn't quite analogous to regaining one's vision, but the words were somehow appropriate. Selling one's soul meant giving up one's identity—and if the operation worked, that was precisely what he'd be doing. The old Benjamin Passmore would cease to exist.

The frightening part was that he had no idea who the new Benjamin Passmore would be.

Sure you do. He'll be a nineteen-year-old high-school senior with unusual taste in music, strange clothes, and a room full of upside-down posters.

He could still change his mind, he realized. He hadn't yet told anyone at home that he was going away—even though he and Nina had come up with an excuse. And he wasn't sure if he was going to tell anyone. It might just be easier to make a quick, unannounced getaway and avoid any awkward questions. Easiest of all would be to cancel the whole trip.

"Woke up this morning, couldn't find my walkin' shoes . . ."

But even as these thoughts raced through his mind, he knew that staying home was out of the question. He couldn't live with himself if he did. It wasn't in his nature to avoid things out of fear. He'd often told himself that he wasn't afraid of *anything*—with the possible exception of losing his hearing, or being attacked by a gang of hoodlums, or making a fool of himself by tripping and falling into a puddle.

He grinned ruefully. At that moment he was also afraid of something else—that Zoey would call Lucas, or vice versa, and that Lucas would tell her that her older brother had gone totally bonkers that afternoon. He supposed he could call Lucas himself, but what would he say? *Hi, Lucas. It's Benjamin. Sorry I freaked out on you this afternoon, but you see, I might regain my vision and I'm really nervous about it, so I'm sneaking off the island tomorrow without telling anyone, and I'd really appreciate it if you kept your mouth shut. Come back for spaghetti anytime.*

Benjamin laughed out loud. It might just be worth it to hear Lucas's reaction. After that, Lucas probably wouldn't ever come back and pressure him for information about Zoey.

He sighed and dropped another shirt in his canvas bag.

"I sold my soul, but I ain't got nothin' to lose . . . "

Eight

After bundling herself in several sweaters, a coat, a hat, and a scarf, Claire climbed up the ladder to her widow's walk. The frigid air made her pause for a second, but she forced herself to continue. At least it wasn't snowing. She'd been out in blizzards that made that night's conditions seem fit for a picnic.

With fingers that were quickly becoming numb, she reached around the chimney to the loose brick where her diary lay hidden. Fortunately, the light of the full moon was easily bright enough for her to see what she was writing.

Temperature: 25 degrees. Winds about five miles per hour. Very clear. The moisture moved north promising more clear skies for tomorrow.

Tonight Nina told me that Benjamin is looking into an operation that could

possibly restore his vision. I don't know
how to feel. Part of me is very happy
for him and praying that everything
works out. Another part of me is
concerned — and not for his health.

Ever since he went blind, Benjamin
has prided himself on the fact that
he can function as well as people who
can see. In certain ways, he can function
better. Blindness is his defining feature.
And odd as it may sound, I think I still
know him well enough to know that he's
feeling very insecure about what will
happen to him if he loses that.

But I can't talk to him about any of
this. Nina insists that I keep it secret.
And I have to do what she says, because
she's his girlfriend now. I can't talk to
anyone about

The pencil slipped. Claire's fingers were too numb to control it well enough to write. It was as if her hand had turned to Silly Putty. She tried sliding the pencil back into the spine of the diary, but she couldn't seem to manage that, either. Finally, in a fit of frustration, she jammed both the diary and the pencil in her coat pocket and descended the ladder to the warmth of her room.

The house was very quiet, except for the faint sound of Nine Inch Nails floating up from Nina's room. At least Claire thought it was Nine Inch Nails. She had a hard time telling apart any of the groups Nina liked.

She stood very still for a moment. There was another sound now—the sound of Nina laughing on the phone. Was she talking to Benjamin? Claire couldn't tell. She could also be talking to Zoey or Aisha.

Cupping her hands in front of her mouth, Claire blew on her fingers in a feeble attempt to warm them. Then she tossed her diary on her desk, shed her coat and hat and scarf, and sat down to continue where she'd left off.

I can't talk to anyone about how I feel about Benjamin. I suppose I could talk to my dad, but it's not quite the same. Besides, Dad's lost in la-la land with Sarah Mendel, the feel-good dwarf of the year.

I guess I shouldn't be so harsh. Dad's happy, and that's the important thing. Also, if Dad weren't involved with Sarah Mendel, Aaron Mendel wouldn't be staying on Chatham Island.

I still can't believe he kissed Zoey. She isn't his type. He's got something

Claire stopped writing and let the pencil clatter to the top of her desk. She leaned back in her chair. Her energy and desire to record her thoughts had rapidly faded, like the sun setting on a winter day.

She heard another laugh downstairs. Nina was still on the phone. Her father still hadn't come home yet. For a moment she was almost tempted to turn on the computer and check in with her old friend Flyer—but she realized that was out of the question. She'd given Sean a clear message when she'd walked out on him at the airport: He wasn't physically attractive enough for her, not even to be her friend.

No, there was nobody to talk to. She was all alone.

Claire had always prized her solitude. Most nights she'd be happy to be by herself.

She only wished it were one of those nights.

* * *

Lucas was just turning off his desk lamp when the phone rang. He picked it up after the second ring. "Hello?"

"Hey, man, it's me."

"Hey, Christopher. What's up?"

"Nothing. I'm just calling to apologize for calling so late last night."

Lucas grinned. "No problem. Just don't make a habit of it. My dad wasn't too psyched. You get everything straightened out with Aisha?"

"You bet." Christopher's voice was brimming with confidence. "Making up is always the best part, dude. You should know that."

"Yeah." Lucas felt a twinge of envy. "I'm looking forward to making up with Zoey one of these days."

"You guys have a fight?"

"Sort of. To tell you the truth, I don't know. All I know is that something's bothering her."

"Well, that's understandable."

Lucas scowled. "It is?"

"Sure. I mean, the whole thing with Benjamin."

"Yeah—something's bothering *him*, too. The whole family's going nuts."

"Come on, dude—you have to admit it's pretty big news." Christopher laughed. "I'm surprised at you. I thought you were supposed to be one of those sensitive guys."

Lucas wrinkled his brow. This conversation wasn't making any sense. He was beginning to get angry— pretty remarkable considering how much energy he'd already spent being pissed off that night. "Christopher, what the hell are you talking about?"

"What do you think I'm taking about? Benjamin's operation."

"Benjamin's *operation?*" Lucas repeated.

The line was quiet for several seconds.

"Christopher?"

"Oh, man," he mumbled. "I think I just made a big mistake."

"Look, you'd better tell me right now what's going on," Lucas demanded. "I'm serious."

There was another moment of silence. "Are you saying you don't know about Benjamin's operation?" Christopher finally asked.

"Of course I don't!" Lucas barked. "What kind of operation? What are you talking about?"

"Aisha will kill me if she finds out I told you," Christopher said nervously. "I just assumed that Zoey must have told you already. I mean, isn't that the way things work with these Chatham Island girls? Eesh tells Nina, Nina tells Zoey, Zoey tells you—"

"Christopher, *I'm* gonna kill you if you don't tell me what's going on. Right this second."

"Oh, man . . . well, I guess it's too late now . . . Benjamin might get some kind of surgery that could restore his sight." The words tumbled awkwardly out of Christopher's mouth. "I just thought you would have known—"

"Are you *sure?*" Lucas interrupted, incredulous.

"That's why he and Aisha were spending so much time together. Aisha was helping him look into it. They had to use the Internet, and I guess she's the only one around here who knows how to do it. He still doesn't know if it's gonna work. He has to have some tests done first. That's why he wants to keep it a secret. He doesn't want to get anyone's hopes up."

"I don't believe it," Lucas mumbled. His initial shock had been replaced by a brief moment of anger that Zoey hadn't told him—then by guilt. No wonder she had been so distracted. No wonder Benjamin had lost his temper.

"You still there?"

"Yeah, I'm still here." Lucas suddenly wished Christopher hadn't called. Now he *knew* why Zoey was acting so strange, but he wasn't in a position to talk to her about it. It would be far better not to know, he realized. Anger was much preferable to guilt.

"Look, man, I'd better go," Christopher said. "You gotta promise me you won't tell anyone you know about this. Especially Aisha."

"I promise." Lucas felt as if he were repeating a ritual he'd performed a thousand times.

"All right," Christopher said reluctantly. "I owe you one, man. I'll talk to you later."

Lucas hung up the phone and put his face in his hands. He figured he'd probably better just go to sleep. He'd need all the rest he could get. The next day was going to be a lousy one.

Friday

6:45 A.M.

Jake sneaks home after having spent the night with Lara and blowing off his paper.

7:05 A.M.

Nina tells Mr. Geiger that she's going to Boston with Benjamin that weekend to see the Boston Philharmonic. Mr. Geiger says that sounds "absolutely wonderful." He informs Claire that the Mendels will be joining them that night for dinner.

7:33 A.M.

Claire and Nina arrive at the ferry. Zoey and Benjamin arrive soon after, followed by Lucas and then by Jake. Nina, Benjamin, and Lucas retire to the cabin. Zoey and Claire huddle together at the front of the deck, even though the temperature is twenty-eight degrees. They discuss their papers on *The Scarlet Letter*. Jake tries to join the conversation and fails miserably.

7:40 A.M.

Aisha barely makes the ferry. She joins Benjamin, Nina, and Lucas downstairs. Jake follows. Aisha tries to start a conversation and fails miserably.

8:05 A.M.

The ferry arrives in Weymouth.

8:25 A.M.

During homeroom, Zoey excuses herself to go to the nurse's office, complaining of an upset stomach. The nurse gives her Maalox and tells her she can skip gym.

9:07 A.M.

Lucas leaves a note in Zoey's locker that reads, *Sorry about last night. I love you.*

10:39 A.M.

Zoey falls asleep in journalism class. Mr. Schwarz, Zoey's favorite teacher, wakes her by hitting her over the head with a copy of the *Weymouth Times.*

11:14 A.M.

Zoey finds Lucas's note in her locker. She runs to the bathroom and vomits.

11:15 A.M.

Aisha and Claire wonder why Zoey is not in gym class.

12:15 P.M.

Nina, Zoey, and Aisha meet for lunch. Nina makes three disgusting jokes about the chicken pot pie, observing the rule of comic tautology, which states that everything funny must come in threes. Zoey tells her to shut up. Aisha tries to make conversation and fails miserably. Lucas, Benjamin, and Jake eat alone, as does Claire.

1:00 P.M.

Jake, Zoey, and Claire arrive in English class. Zoey and Claire hand in their papers. Jake admits he has not finished his. Later he falls asleep in class, as does Zoey.

1:47 P.M.

Lucas arrives in history class, looking for Zoey.

1:53 P.M.

Zoey arrives late and cannot sit next to Lucas.

2:34 P.M.

Lucas walks Zoey to French class and asks if she got his note. Zoey says she hasn't been to her locker all day.

3:20 P.M.

The last bell rings. Zoey tells Lucas she wants to do some shopping at the mall before she goes home. Lucas asks if he can join her. Zoey reluctantly agrees.

4:00 P.M.

Nina, Claire, Benjamin, Jake, and Aisha take the ferry back to Chatham Island. Everyone sits in the cabin. Nobody says a word. Jake falls asleep.

4:25 P.M.
The ferry arrives at Chatham Island. Aisha goes to Christopher's apartment. Claire climbs up to her widow's walk to watch the sunset. Jake passes out in bed. Nina and Benjamin collect their belongings and meet back at the ferry landing.

5:10 P.M.
Claire watches from her widow's walk as the ferry departs for Weymouth, with Nina and Benjamin on board.

Nine

At 5:40 Zoey and Lucas slammed the doors of Zoey's parents' van and pulled out of the Weymouth Mall parking lot. They turned south onto Airport Road, heading back toward the multistory garage where all the islanders kept their "real" cars. "Real" cars, like the van, were automobiles that could actually be used on normal streets, as opposed to "island" cars, which were shabby junk heaps that never made it to the mainland.

The trip had been a disaster from the start. Zoey had intended to get some Christmas shopping done—*alone*, so she could also have some time to think—but Lucas had doggedly insisted on keeping her company. She'd done everything short of telling him to get lost. To make matters worse, he'd been nice to the point of being obsequious, which was very un-Lucas-like. In the end, his presence, coupled with her exhaustion, had made her snappy and irritable—and on more than one occasion, downright mean. Also, she'd ended up buying nothing, an unprecedented occurrence when she went to the mall.

After several minutes of driving in silence, Lucas finally took a deep breath. "Hey, I'm sorry if I got on your nerves this afternoon. I only came because I thought you might like some company.''

Zoey shrugged by way of response, keeping a white-knuckled grip on the steering wheel. Night had long since fallen, and traffic was sluggish.

''Yeah, well, you should have told me you had terminal PMS,'' he muttered.

A laugh escaped her lips. ''There's the old Lucas.''

''What's *that* supposed to mean?''

She glanced at him, then turned back to the road. ''It means I was wondering when you were going to stop being so nice and start acting like yourself again.''

''Oh, right. I'm an insensitive jerk. I must have forgotten.''

Zoey looked at him again. ''That's not what I meant.''

''Of course it is, Zo,'' he said flatly. He shook his head. ''Man, I should have known this was gonna be a nightmare. I should have just kept to myself until . . .'' He let the sentence hang.

''Until what?''

''Forget it.'' He leaned forward and snapped on the radio. The van was instantly filled with the deafening bass and drums of some hip-hop song Zoey had never heard before.

Zoey reached over and turned the volume down. ''Come on, Lucas,'' she said, struggling to maintain her concentration on the road.

''What are you doing?'' Lucas protested. ''That's my favorite song.''

Zoey couldn't help but laugh again. ''I thought you only like songs that feature an emaciated, angst-ridden white male screeching at the top of his lungs.''

"Well, I guess you don't know me as well as you thought," he said coldly. "I sure as hell don't know you as well as *I* thought."

Zoey chewed on her lip. The words stung, but what could she say? They were true. Lucas *didn't* know her as well as he thought.

After a few moments Lucas turned off the radio. "Fine. We'll have it your way. We'll just enjoy the rest of the ride in silence."

The line of cars ahead had come to a standstill. Zoey slowed to a stop.

"Oh, man," Lucas grumbled. "This is perfect."

Zoey leaned back in the driver's seat. She didn't like this any more than he did, but she kept quiet. She knew anything she said would set him off. She stared out the window, trying to figure out why the traffic had stopped. A faint nervousness prickled the back of her neck. They were directly in front of the bus station. This area of Weymouth wasn't exactly the safest part of town. Aside from the lights at the entrance to the station, the rest of the road wasn't very well lit. At least it was crowded. People were filing in and out of the station.

Two figures walking arm in arm up the street suddenly caught her attention. Zoey placed her hands on the side window and squinted at them. One was a girl in a black parka and black hat. The other was a taller boy in a long dark overcoat. Both were carrying bags. Zoey's pulse accelerated. As they drew closer, she saw that the girl had an unlit cigarette in her mouth. The boy was wearing dark glasses.

"Benjamin and Nina!" Zoey cried. The light above the bus station doors illuminated their faces the instant before they disappeared inside.

"What?" Lucas asked.

Zoey turned to him, her mouth hanging open. "I just saw Benjamin and Nina walking into that bus station!"

Lucas cocked an eyebrow. "Come on, Zo, that can't be right . . ."

But Zoey was already fumbling for her seat-belt. Without another thought, she threw the door open and leaped out of the van.

"Zoey!" Lucas called after her. "Wait!"

The entrance opened into a large, noisy room, brightly lit with fluorescent lights. Zoey's heart was pounding. She carefully scanned the crowd. "Benjamin!" she called. "Nina!" A few people gave her odd looks, but there was no sign of Benjamin and Nina.

All at once she heard the angry cacophony of car horns outside the doors.

After one last look, Zoey turned and dashed back outside. The van was still sitting there with the driver's-side door open, but the line of cars in front of it had vanished. Now there was only a line of cars behind it, all of which were honking.

"What are you, crazy?" someone yelled as she hopped back in and slammed the door.

"I don't believe this," she muttered. She put her foot on the gas, and the van lurched forward. "What are they doing? I'm going back there."

"This is a one-way street, Zo," Lucas warned. She could feel his eyes on her. "I wouldn't turn off it. Neither of us knows our way around this part of town very well."

"Lucas, I just saw my brother and my best friend disappear into a bus station. I'm gonna pull over."

"Let them go, Zoey."

She swerved the van over to the left side of the road and screeched to a halt. "Let them go?" she yelled. "What is your problem?"

"It's fairly obvious what they're doing," he said calmly. "I mean, think about it. It makes sense."

"*Obvious?*" Benjamin and Nina could be running away, for all she knew, and Lucas thought it was obvious. Had he lost his mind?

"Zoey, listen to me," he said soothingly, placing his hand on her arm. "I know all about it. And I'm sure there's a logical explanation. They probably didn't want to tell you they were leaving tonight because you'd want to go with them."

"Go *with* them?" she sputtered. "Lucas, you're not making any sense."

"I know about the operation, Zo."

"The *operation?* What are you talking about?"

"What do you think I'm talking about?" He removed his hand. "Benjamin's operation. The one that's gonna restore his vision. The one that's been making you and Benjamin act like escapees from an insane asylum."

Zoey blinked. She couldn't process what Lucas had just said. It was the most ludicrous thing she had ever heard.

"I don't know what's gotten into you," she whispered in a tremulous voice. For some reason her entire body was shaking. She couldn't seem to control herself. She stared at him one last time, then turned and bolted from the car.

For a while Lucas was unable to think. He was unable to do anything but stare blankly at the dashboard. But after Zoey had been gone for a little more than three minutes, he forced himself to accept the meaning of what had transpired.

Zoey hadn't known about Benjamin's operation.

He sighed very deeply. He'd known this was going to be a bad day. But with the exception of the day Jake's brother died, this was easily turning out to be the worst day of his life.

He couldn't understand how this could have happened. How could *Christopher* know and not Zoey, Benjamin's own sister? How could Aisha know . . . well, Aisha knew because she'd been helping Benjamin all along. Lucas nodded slowly. The truth was beginning to dawn on him. Benjamin hadn't wanted anyone besides Aisha to know—but Aisha had told Christopher. And so on.

So much for Christopher's theory about the girls of Chatham Island, he thought glumly. *The boys are just as bad.*

Right then all he could do was pray that Zoey caught them before they got on the bus. The only thing that could possibly make this day worse would be having to explain everything to Zoey himself—which meant explaining why Benjamin hadn't wanted to tell her about the surgery. This part would be difficult, since Lucas really had no idea.

The driver's-side door suddenly opened. "They're gone," Zoey said quietly. She climbed in, then sat for a moment and glowered at Lucas. "So you want to tell me what this is all about?"

He just hung his head. *Haven't you learned by now, Lucas? You should always know to expect the worst.*

"I guess I don't have a choice," he said as she started the car.

"No. You don't."

Another thought occurred to him then. If Zoey hadn't known about Benjamin's operation, then something else had been bothering her all this time. Something totally unrelated.

Of course, now was probably not the best time to ask what it was.

Ten

Buses were definitely *not* Nina's favorite mode of transportation. For starters, they always smelled like a combination of dirty laundry and bathroom disinfectant. And the seats were always too small and cramped. She knew her butt would be falling asleep in less than an hour.

The bus was just pulling onto Interstate 95. Nina groaned, staring out the window into the night. At least six hours until Boston—that's what the driver had said. Her butt would probably fall off by that point.

"I swear I heard Zoey calling our names right before we got on," Benjamin suddenly announced.

"Ooh," she said. "Spooky."

Benjamin grimaced. "No, really."

She put her hand on his knee and brought her lips close to his ear. "Well, I wasn't gonna tell you, but I think I saw Elvis back there. Or maybe it was Jimmy Hoffa. Of course, it could have been that pesky Lindbergh baby."

"Nina, I'm serious."

"So am I."

For a moment Benjamin's lips remained pressed in

a tight line. Then he burst out laughing. "Why do you always do that?"

"Do what?"

"Get me really mad—then make me laugh?"

"Because your two cutest expressions are those of unbridled fury and humorous abandon," she answered.

Benjamin lifted an eyebrow over the rim of his dark glasses. "I guess that's a good thing to know." He put his hand over hers, then leaned back in his seat.

Nina turned back to the window, thankful he'd left it at that. She'd thought she'd heard Zoey back there, too, but she'd dismissed it as far too improbable. Besides, they'd been running late, so it wasn't as if they could have stopped to check. Even if it *had* been Zoey, there wasn't anything they could do about it now. She was bound to find out sooner or later—especially since Benjamin had just left without telling anyone.

Benjamin's decision to leave secretly had been an odd one. Nina still felt it was unfair of Benjamin not to tell Zoey, but at least she could understand his reasons. She couldn't understand why he'd just run away without any kind of excuse. The Passmores were bound to get worried. Then they'd call Nina's place looking for them. Then Nina's dad would tell them that she and Benjamin had gone to Boston to see the Philharmonic. The Passmores, having brains, would suspect foul play—and they'd press each and every one of the island kids for the truth until Aisha finally cracked. Nina could see the whole thing unfolding like a well-choreographed dance. She sighed. Chatham Island was way too predictable.

"What are you thinking?" Benjamin asked.

"I'm thinking that by the time we get back, everyone's gonna know why we left."

"I know."

"You don't sound too worried about it."

"I'm not. I planned it that way."

"You *what*?"

He shrugged. "Eesh has probably told someone else by now—Christopher or maybe even Zoey. But even if she hasn't, my parents are gonna wonder why I'm gone—and knowing them as I do, I know they're gonna find out the truth." He grinned. "We Chatham Island folks aren't very good at keeping secrets."

Nina was glad Benjamin couldn't see her right then, because she knew she looked extremely guilty. He still had no idea that she'd told Claire. "So what made you plan it that way?" she asked.

"Because you were right, as usual. People *do* have a right to know. This doesn't affect just me. But I know if I told everyone now, my parents and Zoey would want to come, and I just don't feel like being at the center of some big production. You see . . . my dad has always felt this weird kind of guilt ever since the whole thing happened. It's stupid, but I know he'd be freaking out. And besides . . ." He paused. "Besides, I wanted to be alone with you this weekend," he finished quietly.

Now Nina was *really* glad Benjamin couldn't see her, because she was blushing. She'd been thinking about being alone with him as well. But this wasn't exactly the most romantic occasion.

"You have to admit, our last road trip together wasn't a huge success," he added.

"What are you talking about?" she exclaimed.

"Lots of people would kill for a chance to get stuck in the mud and wander into the middle of a Satanic ritual—only to find out it was actually a documentary on witchcraft."

"Jeez, when you put it *that* way . . . ," Benjamin said dryly.

"Maybe we'll get lucky again." Nina pulled the pack of Lucky Strikes from her pocket and shoved one in her mouth. "Maybe we'll have to check into some seedy motel where the manager is really skinny and keeps talking about his mother."

"And has a habit of attacking helpless women in the shower with a knife?" Benjamin suggested.

"Nah—a knife would be too obvious. I was thinking more along the lines of a Nerf football, or a croquet mallet, or a big, mushy tomato."

"Now *there's* a scary movie."

Nina took a drag of her cigarette. "So what names should we use when we check in?"

"Names?"

"You know—we're gonna need aliases."

"We are?" he asked with a smile.

"Well, not really. But I think we should use them anyway." She paused. "I wonder what my dad and the midget use."

Benjamin laughed. "Ms. Mendel is staying at the Grays', remember? It's not a scandalous secret. My guess is that she uses her own name."

"Staying at the Grays' is only a recent development. When they were first seeing each other, I bet they met at some cheap motel in Weymouth during lunch breaks—" She broke off and made a face. "Ugh. I'm gonna make myself hurl."

"Maybe we should check in under the name Mr. and Mrs. Mendel—"

An elderly woman suddenly poked her head around the back of Benjamin's seat. "Excuse me, miss," she said crossly. "There's no smoking on the bus."

"I'm not smoking, ma'am," Nina said as politely as she could manage.

"Well, what do you intend to do with that cigarette?" the woman demanded.

"Just what I'm doing now, ma'am," Nina replied cheerfully. "Enjoying that cool Lucky Strike flavor without the hazards of lung cancer or heart disease."

The woman snorted. After a quick, disdainful look at both Nina and Benjamin, she withdrew her head.

Benjamin leaned toward Nina. "You oughta be in Lucky Strike commercials," he whispered. "Your voice is perfect: sexy and very convincing."

"Well, you know my lifelong dream has always been to do cartoon voice-overs—"

Benjamin placed his lips over hers. Nina was grateful to stop talking. Not only was she making a fool of herself, but his mention of *Mr. and Mrs.* had gotten her blushing again.

Kissing also helped one forget that one's butt was falling asleep.

Zoey was barely conscious of saying good-bye to Lucas at the ferry landing. She marched straight to her parents' restaurant. According to Lucas, her parents didn't know anything about Benjamin's plans, either. She couldn't remember ever having been so angry. Apparently half the island knew, but Benjamin's own family didn't.

Instead of walking through the front door, she decided it would be better to go through the alley off Dock Street and into the kitchen. That way she could avoid any kind of scene in front of the customers— although she doubted it would matter. Everybody eating dinner there probably knew about Benjamin's operation as well.

"Zoey!" her father exclaimed as she burst into the tiny stainless-steel kitchen area. He was hovering over a large pot on the stove, slowly stirring a thick, bubbly tomato sauce. His white apron, tied tightly around a tie-dyed T-shirt, was already covered with bright red splotches.

Zoey's eyes immediately flashed to Christopher, who was standing at the counter with his back to her, peeling garlic. "Hey, Zo," he called over his shoulder. "How's it going?"

"Christopher, would you mind getting out of here for a few minutes? I've got something I need to talk about with my dad."

Mr. Passmore stopped stirring. His playful blue eyes lost their sparkle. "Zoey, are you all right?" he asked worriedly.

"I'm fine, I'm fine," she said, keeping her eyes fixed on Christopher.

"I'll be back in a few, Mr. P.," he mumbled, undoing the ties at the back of his apron. He glanced furtively between Zoey and her father. "I'll just take a little walk."

"Don't worry about it." Mr. Passmore shook his head. "We can manage without you. It's slow for a Friday. Go on—go have some fun."

Christopher paused in the doorway as he put on his coat. "You sure? I just got here."

"I'm sure." He forced a smile. "Thanks for all your help tonight."

Christopher looked at Zoey one last time, then closed the door behind him.

"So what's this all about?" Mr. Passmore asked, wiping his hands on his apron, then tightening the band on his ponytail. He moved back to the pot on the stove and began stirring again.

"Dad, do you know anything about Benjamin?"

He laughed confusedly. "Uh . . . sure. I think so. I'm his father, after all."

"That's not what I meant," Zoey snapped. "I mean, has he ever mentioned anything about an operation?"

Mr. Passmore looked at her with an expression of bewilderment. "Operation? No, I don't think so. Zoey, will you please tell me what's going on?"

"Benjamin just got on a bus to Boston. He's going to the hospital there to have some tests done. Apparently there's some new kind of experimental surgery that can reverse blindness."

Mr. Passmore dropped his spoon into the sauce. For a moment he just gaped at her. Then he blinked rapidly a few times. "Boston?" he finally managed.

Zoey nodded, taken off guard. That hadn't been the response she'd been expecting. She'd been expecting something more along the lines of "Oh, my God!" or "This is insane!"—or maybe just an appropriate obscenity.

"When did you find out about this?" he asked.

"Just now. Lucas and I were coming back from the mall, and we got stuck in traffic right in front of the bus station. I just happened to see Benjamin walk into the station with Nina." She threw her hands up in exasperation. "If there hadn't been a traffic jam, I wouldn't even *know* right now."

Mr. Passmore leaned back against the counter and nodded slowly, stroking his chin. His youthful, vibrant features suddenly looked very old and tired. "Did, uh . . . did you get a chance to talk to him?"

Zoey shook her head. "I chased after him, but they were already gone. Lucas told me everything on the way back."

"Lucas?" He frowned. "Lucas knows about this?"

Zoey laughed bitterly. "Actually, Christopher told him. And Eesh told Christopher. Eesh was the one who found out first. Everyone seems to know except us."

"Man, oh, man." He chewed on a fingernail. "You say Nina is with him?"

"Yeah."

"Good," he said distractedly. "At least he's not alone."

"Not alone?" Zoey yelled. "Is that what you're worried—"

"Zoey, relax, all right?" he interrupted. "Getting worked up isn't gonna do anybody any good."

The swinging door that connected the kitchen to the rest of the restaurant opened a crack, revealing a mane of blond hair. "I thought I heard your voice," Mrs. Passmore said with an awkward smile at Zoey. "Is everything all right in here?"

"You'd better come on in," Mr. Passmore said. "We've got some interesting news."

Mrs. Passmore looked behind her, then reluctantly slipped through the door. "You know I shouldn't leave the customers alone."

"Darla, Benjamin is on his way to Boston right now," he announced.

She looked at Zoey, then back at him. Her eyes narrowed. "You want to run that by me again?"

Mr. Passmore gestured toward Zoey. "Maybe she should tell you."

Zoey sighed, looking at the floor to avoid her mom's eyes. "He's going to Boston General Hospital to look into some kind of surgery that can reverse blindness." She felt as if she'd said those exact words a hundred times in the last hour.

"Good Lord." Mrs. Passmore put her her hand over her mouth. "Why . . . why didn't he tell us?"

"The *rumor* is, he didn't want to get anyone's hopes up." Zoey shrugged. "But then again, I have no idea. I just found out myself."

Mrs. Passmore shifted from one foot to the other. "This is . . . this is . . ." She ran a hand through her hair. "Look—I can't even think right now. We'll talk about it at home tonight." She shot an unreadable look at Mr. Passmore, then exited the room.

"Good old Mom," Zoey muttered caustically. "She always has the perfect solution for these touchy situations."

"That's *enough*, Zoey," Mr. Passmore stated, glaring at her. "Your mother's right. There's nothing we can do about it now. We'll talk about it when we get home—as a family."

"A family?" Whenever her dad mentioned the word *family* these days, he inevitably meant that Lara would somehow be involved. "You mean Lara, too?"

"Of course I mean Lara," Mr. Passmore snapped. He grabbed a large soup ladle off the wall and used it to extract the spoon that had fallen into the sauce.

"Listen, I know you're upset." He softened his tone. "But sitting around here yelling at each other isn't really going to accomplish anything, is it?"

"Well, I know how we can accomplish something." Zoey folded her arms across her chest. "We can go to the Weymouth airport tonight and get on a flight to Boston."

Her father looked toward the ceiling for a moment, then put the ladle and spoon down. He walked over to her and gently placed his hands on her shoulders. "Zoey, even if we could afford to do that, I wouldn't want to. Benjamin made a decision to do this by himself. He's nineteen years old. I don't know why he did this, but I have to respect his decision."

Zoey wriggled free of her dad's grasp. "That's the biggest load of crap I ever heard!"

Too flustered to form another coherent sentence, she turned and stormed out the door.

JAKE

What is my deepest, darkest secret? Wow. I have a lot to choose from. Nobody knows I'm seeing Lara, but I'm pretty sure Benjamin and Lucas suspect something's up. The way things are going between us, it won't be a secret for long.

It might be that I'm an alcoholic. But maybe that's not really a secret, either. Everybody has seen me drunk at one time or another. A few people have even told me that they're worried about me, which is one of the reasons I promised myself that I'm never going to drink again.

I guess I'd have to say that right now, my deepest, darkest secret is that I saw my brother, Wade, on Halloween night. Lara says the whole thing with the Ouija board was a sham, but I know what I saw. He was there. "Just live" was the last thing he said to me after he told me I was going to join him if I didn't stop drinking.

I think all of my secrets are maybe just part of one big secret that I haven't quite figured out yet.

Eleven

Jake's eyelids fluttered. He was aware that he was lying in bed and that it was dark—but not much else. There was a ringing sound.

The phone. Jake groggily rolled over and fumbled for the receiver. "Hello?" he moaned.

"Hi, Jakie. Miss me today?"

"Lara." His voice was gravelly. He felt disoriented, as though he knew he shouldn't be asleep right at that moment. "Hey—what time is it?"

A laugh exploded into his ear so loudly that he jerked. "I don't know what time it is," she said in a lilting, singsong voice. "I think around seven. Who cares? It's Friday night."

Something in the way she spoke set off an alarm in his mind. He sat up in bed, instantly alert. "Lara, have you been drinking?"

"Noooo."

"Lara—"

"Okay, maybe just a couple of sips. But that's it."

"A couple of sips of what?" he demanded.

"Tequila." She giggled. "Your favorite."

"Stay right there. I'm coming over." He could

hear her laughing as he slammed the phone down on the hook.

This is bad. This is so bad. . . .

Shivering, he leaped out of the bed and shoved his feet into his boots. His mind was racing. Her problem must have been a lot bigger than he'd realized. It all made perfect sense now: the way she abruptly changed personalities as if she were flipping a switch, the way she couldn't tell right from wrong. She was probably out of her mind with alcoholism.

He hastily pulled on his jacket and yanked open the sliding glass doors of his bedroom. The temperature was well below freezing, but he took a deep breath and scurried up the hill to the front of his house without bothering with the jacket zipper. Running to the Passmores' would warm him up soon enough.

Hang on, Lara.

Leeward Drive was deserted. Jake could hear the ocean waves crashing in the blackness as he sprinted down the middle of the road. His boots pounded the pavement in precise, measured steps. It felt good to be moving so fast.

The uneven cobblestones slowed his pace slightly as he veered right on South Street, then right again on Camden—but he was already there. The Passmores' dark house loomed in front of him. At least nobody else was home. His heart bounced as he climbed the garage stairs and threw open Lara's door.

"Jakie!" she cried. "Man, that was fast! You're like some kinda . . . some kinda superhero or something."

Jake surveyed the room. Lara was sprawled across her mattress. Her eyes were unfocused, and her hair and clothes were in disarray. A half-empty bottle of tequila stood at the foot of the bed.

"Did you drink *all* of that tonight?" He took two quick steps forward and snatched the bottle off the floor.

"No, silly. Some of it I drank before." She rolled over and gazed up at him. "The rest I'm saving for a rainy day—unless you want it."

Jake caught a whiff of the pungent, sour smell from the bottle. His stomach clenched. For a moment he wondered if he was going to be sick. He held the bottle at arm's length, thinking about the last time he'd drunk tequila. It had been Halloween night. . . .

"Come on, Jakie," she whispered. "One sip isn't gonna kill you. It's the weekend. Time to let loose."

"What about two nights ago?" he demanded. "You told me you had a problem. You swore to me you were never gonna drink again."

She laughed. "I was crossing my . . . crossing my fingers. Come on, jus' this one las' time," she slurred.

"You could have called me," he spat, suddenly disgusted. "You said you would call me."

"I *did* call you." She reached out and put an unsteady hand on his leg. Her T-shirt came out of her jeans in the process. He could see her belly button now. The faint outline of her bra was plainly visible through the thin white fabric of the shirt. He quickly averted his eyes, concentrating hard on not noticing how good she looked.

"Come on," she pleaded. "Just one las' sip, for old times' sake."

He shook his leg free of her hand and marched over to the door.

"Hey—whaddaya doin'?"

"I'm taking this with me," he said, clutching the bottle tightly. "Just turn off the light and go to sleep, Lara."

"You *bastard*!" she shrieked. She grabbed the pillow and tried to throw it at him, but it wound up falling to the floor next to her bed.

"You're a sick girl," Jake said in a shaky, hollow voice. "I want to help you, but I can't when you're like this."

"You don't want to *help* me." Suddenly Lara burst into tears. "You just want me to show you a good time. Just like Keith. Just like everyone else. Get 'em loaded and bang 'em. That's all you . . ." The last words were lost in a fit of convulsive sobs.

Jake cringed. He didn't want to hear any more of this terrible drunken confession. But part of him wanted to run over and hug her and console her—to reassure her that he wasn't like her old boyfriend or anyone else with whom she'd been involved before. The other part of him knew it was pointless to try to talk to her just then. He doubted if she'd remember anything anyway.

"Lara, I'm going," he said finally. He raised his voice in an effort to be heard over her weeping. "Please just try to get some sleep."

She didn't respond.

Clutching the bottle tightly, Jake walked around the room and turned off all the lights, then quickly descended the stairs.

All that hippie garbage has finally gone to his head, Zoey thought miserably. *I might as well have Wavy Gravy for a father.*

She kept her head nuzzled into her coat to protect

102

herself from the wind as she marched down South Street toward Camden. For once, the foul weather matched her mood.

She could tolerate his father's newfound love for his mother and their touchy-feely, I'm-okay-you're-okay relationship. It was embarrassing, but she could tolerate it. She could even tolerate the fact that he'd opened their home to some love child he'd spawned in the mountains of Italy or wherever it had been. It was hard, it was awkward—but she could manage if it meant keeping the family together.

But she *couldn't* tolerate irresponsibility—especially when it came to Benjamin.

Why couldn't she just have normal parents? Normal parents weren't "buddies" with their children. They didn't go around "respecting" their children's decisions. Normal parents got mad. They took action. They demanded explanations, they meted out punishments, and they hopped on planes when their kids ran away.

Zoey paused when she turned right onto Camden. She squinted through the darkness at her house. Somebody had just left the garage and was walking across the gravel. But it wasn't Lara; it was definitely a boy—a boy wearing a baseball cap and holding what looked like a bottle in his hand. A *familiar* boy. Suddenly the boy froze.

"Jake?" Zoey asked.

"Oh, man . . ."

Zoey walked toward him, trying to make sense out of the scene before her. Jake was standing in front of her house, holding a bottle half-filled with some kind of clear liquid. His face looked sickly in the pale light of the street lamp.

"Jake—what are you *doing* here?" she asked.

"It's not what you think . . . ," he began.

Zoey's eyes widened when she saw the label on the bottle. "Tequila?" she asked in disbelief. "Jake . . ."

"It's not mine," he said. "It's—it's Lara's."

"It's Lara's," she repeated dully. Once again, for about the fifth time that day, she felt nauseated. Had she somehow entered a bad *Twilight Zone* rerun? Benjamin had run away from home with Nina, and her father didn't seem to care. Now Jake—Jake McRoyan, the boy whom she had loved for almost four years of her life—was involved in a drunken rendezvous with her demented half sister. What next? Would Lucas be getting a sex change?

"Zoey, you gotta believe me," Jake begged.

She took a deep breath and looked him in the eye. "You have to admit, it's kind of hard, seeing as you're holding the bottle."

"I took it from Lara. To do this." He walked over to the side of the road and flipped the bottle upside down, letting the contents pour out onto the ground. "I swear I haven't had a drop."

Zoey watched him. He certainly didn't seem drunk; she'd seen him drunk enough times to know the difference. But he looked scared—and guilty. He was hiding *something*. "How did you know that Lara would be drinking right now? Lucky guess?"

"She called me," Jake said simply. He shook the last drops free and tucked the empty bottle into his pocket, then turned to face her.

"I didn't know . . . she had your number."

He shrugged. "Now you know."

The next thing Zoey knew, she was laughing hys-

104

terically. It was pretty strange, considering that the world seemed to be falling apart before her eyes. But she couldn't help it. She felt as if she were watching someone else.

Jake wasn't amused. In fact, he looked frightened. "Hey, Zoey, are you okay?"

"Um, not really," she said, struggling to gain control of herself. "It's just that I've, uh, made a lot of interesting discoveries this evening."

He nodded sympathetically. "You found out about Benjamin."

"*You* know, too?" she cried. She shook her head. "Jeez . . . well, I guess I should have expected it. Who told *you*?"

"Lara, actually."

"Lara. Well. This is perfect." Zoey was no longer laughing; rage was boiling within her again. "How did she know?"

"She overheard him talking to Eesh . . . look, Zoey, it doesn't matter. You just have to promise me something. Promise me you'll do me a favor."

"I don't know, Jake," she muttered. "I'm not in the most generous mood right now."

"I just need you to promise me that you won't tell your parents about this. Just tell them that you came home and found Lara sick in bed. Tell them she went to sleep really early and that she doesn't want to be disturbed."

Zoey looked at him. *This is Jake*, she suddenly realized. Poor, sweet, honest Jake—the one who always tried to do the right thing, the *moral* thing. He was just trying to help a friend—someone who was in the same kind of trouble he'd been in many times himself. Her anger began to subside, leaving only a wistful sadness in its place. Even though she no longer harbored any kind of romantic feelings for him, she still cared about him very much. He never changed. He was always just simple, decent Jake: nothing more or less.

"I think I can do that," she said quietly. "But I need a favor in return."

"What's that?" he asked, looking nervous.

"I need you to give me a hug."

A melancholy smile curled on his lips. "That's a favor? I wouldn't call it that."

She stepped forward and took him in her arms, burying her face in his shoulder. They embraced for what seemed like a long, long time.

Finally they stepped apart.

For the first time all day, Zoey actually felt okay. Not great—but okay. It was amazing how nice okay could feel after a day like the one she'd just had.

Christopher

WHAT IS MY DEEPEST, DARKEST SECRET? HA.
I'M NOT SURE IF I LIKE THAT TERMINOLOGY.
"DEEPEST, DARKEST" IMPLIES THAT THE SECRET
IS BAD, RIGHT? IT MEANS THAT YOU'RE
ASHAMED OR THAT YOU HAVE SOMETHING TO
HIDE. I HAVE A SECRET, BUT I'M NOT ASHAMED
OF IT. THE EXACT OPPOSITE IS TRUE: I'M
PROUD OF IT. IT REPRESENTS THE BEST
DECISION I'VE EVER MADE IN MY LIFE.

   I'M GOING TO ASK AISHA TO MARRY ME.
   MAN. I ACTUALLY SAID THE WORDS. IT'S
STILL PRETTY HARD TO BELIEVE. I MEAN, I'VE
PRETTY MUCH SPENT MY ENTIRE POSTADOLESCENT
LIFE AVOIDING ANY SERIOUS COMMITMENT.
I'VE ALWAYS KEPT MY OPTIONS OPEN. AFTER ALL,
A MAN DOESN'T WANT TO GET TIED DOWN WHEN
HE'S GOT SO MUCH TO OFFER, RIGHT?

   WELL, THAT'S WHAT I USED TO THINK,
ANYWAY, BEFORE I MET AISHA. I GUESS YOU
COULD SAY THAT SHE CHANGED MY LIFE. I KNOW
SHE SAVED IT. IF IT WEREN'T FOR HER, I
PROBABLY WOULD HAVE GONE AHEAD AND PUT A
BULLET THROUGH THE SKULL OF THAT NAZI
PUNK. BUT WHEN MY FINGER WAS ON THE
TRIGGER, PICTURING HER FACE MADE ME
REALIZE JUST HOW MUCH I'D BE THROWING
AWAY. IT MADE ME REALIZE JUST HOW LUCKY I
WAS TO HAVE HER, AND THAT I NEVER, EVER
WANTED TO LOSE HER.

Now comes the hard part. I've decided to join the army. Oh, yeah—that's another secret. The only problem is that if I join the army, I'll have to leave Chatham Island for a long time. Two years, at least.

At first I was worried because that meant leaving Aisha alone with Benjamin. But even after I realized that there was no way Aisha could fall for Benjamin when she had me (no offense, Benjamin), I knew I couldn't stand to be without her. That's what clinched the decision.

So all I need to do is buy the ring and pop the question. Easy, right? Then she says yes, and off we go. It's true I'll miss a lot of the people around here—but I know that if I'm with Aisha, I'll always be coming back.

And if she says no?

To be perfectly honest, I haven't really considered that option.

Twelve

The moment Christopher walked into his room, he picked up the phone and savagely punched in Lucas's number. He didn't even bother taking his jacket off. He had to talk to Lucas. Right away.

After three long rings, he heard a click as the other phone was picked up. "Hello?" Lucas's voice answered.

"You told Zoey, didn't you?" he demanded.

"Fine, thanks, Christopher," Lucas answered sarcastically. "How about you?"

"This is serious, man. I'm not playing."

"Believe me, I know," Lucas said, suddenly sounding deadly serious himself.

"What happened? I told you Aisha would kill me—"

"We saw Benjamin and Nina at the bus station. I figured Zoey already knew. That's how it sounded, the way I heard it from you."

Christopher hesitated. Lucas had a point. Until that afternoon, Christopher *had* thought that Zoey knew. For some reason Aisha had neglected to give him that important piece of information the day before.

109

"Christopher? Look, I'm sorry if I got you in any trouble with Eesh, all right?"

"Ah, don't worry about it. It'll be cool." He laughed once. "I was actually just pissed because Zoey told me to get lost, and Mr. P. said I shouldn't bother coming back."

"He *fired* you?"

"No, no—nothing like that. He just meant I should take the rest of the night off. The thing is, I really need the money right now. But I guess he could tell by the look on Zoey's face that it was gonna be bad."

"Yeah," Lucas said coldly. "Well, he was right about that."

"You all right, man?" Christopher asked. "You sound kind of weird."

"To tell you the truth, no. I'm not all right."

Christopher began to wish he hadn't picked up the phone and yelled in Lucas's ear so quickly. He sounded pretty upset. "You and Zoey still on the rocks?" he asked hesitantly.

"I guess so."

"Hey, you mind if I ask you a question?"

"As long as it's not about how sexually frustrated I am at the moment, no."

Christopher laughed. "Well, it's not totally unrelated." He took a deep breath, thinking through exactly how he wanted to phrase this. "Do you . . . ever think about where you and Zoey are gonna be in a few years?"

"What do you mean?"

"I mean . . . if you'll still be going out."

"The way things stand right now, I don't even know if we'll still be going out next week," Lucas mumbled. "Why?"

"Well, I was just thinking about it today, you know?" Christopher said casually. "I mean, Eesh is graduating this year, and I know she wants to go to college."

"So?"

"So . . . I'm just thinking about what'll happen when she leaves."

"Why? You planning on asking her to marry you or something?"

Christopher's heart abruptly plummeted to the bottom of his stomach. His mouth worked spasmodically, but he couldn't get any words out.

"It's a joke, Christopher. You still there?"

"I—uh—yeah . . . I mean, of course I'm not gonna ask her to *marry* me or anything."

Nice job, he said to himself angrily. *You sound about as convincing as a used-car salesman.*

There was a pause at the other end. "Uh-oh," Lucas said. "I don't know if I can deal with hearing this right now."

"Hearing what?"

"You're serious, aren't you? I mean, you're really gonna ask her to marry you?"

"So what if I am?" Christopher barked defiantly, not caring anymore. It wasn't as if it were *that* crazy. Teenagers got married all the time. Besides, they were both responsible, consenting adults, and they were very much in love. True, they hadn't slept together yet—but in a way, that was more romantic. Even Christopher could appreciate that.

"I—I don't know what to say," Lucas stammered.

"Well, you'd better not say a damn thing," Christopher warned. "Or I'll personally see to it that you won't be opening your mouth ever again."

"Of course not." Lucas cleared his throat. "I guess congratulations are in order."

"Don't jump the gun. I haven't even bought the ring yet."

There was yet another pause. "You—uh—you mind if I ask you a question?"

"Depends on the question," Christopher replied.

"Have you ever thought about how *young* you guys are? I mean, don't take this the wrong way— but why push it? You've got your whole life in front of you. I mean, this is *big*. It's like Benjamin getting his sight back. It's permanent, rest-of-your-life kind of big."

"I know. But I can't afford to wait." There was no reason to hold anything back from Lucas at this point. "I'm joining the army."

"Whoa."

"It makes perfect sense for me, Lucas. I'm strapped for cash, and the pay is great. I'll earn money for college. Plus I get to travel, and learn things like how to use a computer, and get in really good shape." He almost felt as if he were trying to convince himself as much as he was trying to convince Lucas.

"Sounds great," Lucas said doubtfully.

"The only problem is that I'll have to leave. For a long time."

"So you want Aisha to go with you."

"Exactly."

"Well, I've got to hand it to you, Christopher. You're a hell of a lot braver than I am. I guess the only thing left to say is good luck."

"That's it?" Christopher chuckled. "I expected a little more. I thought you affluent white kids always had some witty remark or clever aphorism you saved up for a time like this.''

''Let me tell you something, Christopher,'' Lucas said tiredly. ''You're talking to the wrong white kid.''

Claire listlessly pushed at the food on her plate with her fork, wondering when this dinner was ever going to end. The conversation had been excruciatingly boring all night. Now Sarah, Aaron, and her father were all chattering about some book they'd read recently—going into all kinds of BS about allegories and magical realism. She'd just written an essay on *The Scarlet Letter*, for God's sake. She'd done her literary exercise for the week.

''. . . don't you think, Claire?'' Sarah asked.

''Excuse me?'' She forced a polite smile. ''I'm sorry, I didn't hear the question.''

''Oh—the poor dear!'' Sarah chirped, making a ridiculous pouty face that reminded Claire of a five-year-old. ''We're being so rude.''

''No, no, it's fine,'' Claire said. ''I guess I'm just not as well read as the rest of you.''

''Well, you're still young, sweetie,'' Mr. Geiger said, beaming foolishly. ''There's plenty of time to read.'' He pushed himself from the table and stood. ''I think I'm going to give Janelle the word that we're almost ready for dessert.''

''Burke, please tell her that it was another scrumptious meal,'' Sarah said.

Scrumptious?

''Oh, I will,'' he said. ''She'll be so pleased.''

Claire kept her own smile plastered on her face as her father walked by, but inside she was seething. *There's plenty of time to read*, he had said. He might as well have said, *We all know you're an airhead, but at least you look nice*. He was seriously beginning to get on her nerves. When would the old, somber, predictable Burke Geiger come back to get rid of this bubbly clown?

"Claire," Sarah said, "Aaron tells me that you're quite interested in the weather."

"Meteorology and climatology, yes," Claire answered. Not "*the weather*."

"Well, that sounds fascinating." She giggled. "I've always been a stargazer myself."

Claire nodded. Her eyes flashed briefly to Aaron, but he was wearing the same unreadable grin as his mother.

"You know, I saw something interesting on the news last night," Aaron said after a moment. "The weatherman was talking about how everyone had predicted snow for today—but the low-pressure system, which originated in the Caribbean, was forced to the north." He paused and looked at Claire meaningfully. "It's amazing to me how the atmosphere in one part of the world can so dramatically affect another part."

Claire blinked. It was a pretty stunning performance, she had to admit. He'd spoken those words with such earnest sincerity that she half expected him to launch into a sermon on how weather patterns were a manifestation of God. He'd obviously done his homework since the last time they'd met.

"Looks like you two have something in common," Sarah pronounced happily.

"I guess we do," Claire said, continuing to meet Aaron's gaze. *Yes, we have something in common: We both have a gift for playing roles and turning on the charm at all the right moments. For Zoey, you're the*

114

sexy, mysterious new guy in town. For Sarah and my dad, you're the scholar. And now for me, you've suddenly become the weatherman.

Mr. Geiger returned to the room, and Aaron finally looked away—his face once again becoming a suave, inscrutable mask of amiability.

Who are you really, Aaron Mendel?

Zoey was just beginning to drift off to sleep when she heard the latch of the front door click, signaling her parents' arrival. She yawned, then sat up in bed and rubbed her eyes. The clock read ten-thirty. She was grateful it was so late. At long last this nightmarish day was drawing to a close.

"Zoey?" her father called. "Lara? We're home."

Lara. Zoey immediately hopped out of bed and hurried down the stairwell. "Shhh," she whispered as she met her parents in the front hall. "Lara has some kind of stomach virus or food poisoning or something. She's pretty sick."

"She is?" Mr. Passmore asked worriedly. He hung up his coat in the front hall closet, then took his wife's coat and hung it up for her. "Does she need anything?"

"No, I don't think so." Zoey shook her head. "She told me she just wants to sleep right now. She said she'd let us know if she wants something."

"Hmmm." Mr. Passmore looked dubious.

"We'll check on her in the morning, Jeff," Mrs. Passmore said. "We wouldn't want to wake her up. Sleep is the best thing for stomach bugs. They usually don't last too much longer than the night, anyway. She probably just wants to be alone."

"Yeah, okay." He nodded. "I guess you're right."

Zoey contained a smile as the three of them walked to the kitchen. *You owe me one, sister*, she thought. *Big time*.

"Well, well," Mr. Passmore said dryly, leaning against the refrigerator. "It seems as if we've all had a chance to calm down a bit since our last family meeting. Good."

Zoey slumped into a chair at the table. "I still think we should go to Boston. We can get on a bus tomorrow morning."

"And just close the restaurant?" Mrs. Passmore asked. She sat across from Zoey. "I know you're worried about your brother, but I agree with your father. Chasing after Benjamin isn't going to do anyone any good."

Zoey just sighed. At this point she was too exhausted and too emotionally drained to summon any more anger.

"You know, I think I know why we were all so upset," Mr. Passmore said. "We were upset because we're mad at Benjamin."

"Mad at Benjamin?" Zoey glanced at her father. "I know *I'm* not mad at him. That's your job. You're the parents."

Mr. Passmore gave her a wry little smile. "We're *all* mad at him because he didn't tell us about this—and because he chose to go to Boston with his girlfriend instead of his family. He hurt our feelings. I think we're all feeling a bit shafted."

"Shafted." Zoey laughed. "Give me a break, Dad."

"Well, I know I am," he said seriously. "One of the loneliest times in a parent's life comes when a child starts making decisions without consulting the parent first. You can't help but feel like, 'Oh, so you don't need me anymore.' It's stupid, but we can't help it. Now is one of those times.''

Zoey rolled her eyes. "Uh-oh. I feel another lecture about personal freedom and the counterculture coming on."

Mrs. Passmore laughed. "But he's *right*, Zoey," she said gently. "You're feeling a version of the same thing, too, because Benjamin is your brother. You're thinking: 'Why would he tell Nina and not me?' "

"I—" Zoey was going to refute her mother, but she found she couldn't. Was she really mad? Was she really that petty?

"Think about it, Zo," her father said. "There's absolutely no reason for us to be angry or upset, except that our egos may be slightly bruised. But that's not what's important. *We're* not at issue. Benjamin might be on the verge of a miracle here. This is fantastic news. If we're feeling anything, we should be feeling hopeful and excited. We shouldn't be so self-centered."

"But . . ." Zoey tried to swallow. Her mouth was suddenly very dry. "But what if it doesn't work out?"

Zoey's father walked over to her and put his arm on her shoulder. "If it doesn't work out, we'll be here for Benjamin—to support him and comfort him. I have no doubt that we'll be able to do it."

Zoey nodded. A hard lump had formed in her throat. She couldn't even conceive of how crushing it would be for Benjamin if the operation failed—or if he made the trip only to find that he wasn't even eligible. What was going through his mind at that moment?

"Well, I don't know about you all, but I'm beat,"

Mr. Passmore said, stretching. He kissed Zoey on the top of the head and left the kitchen. "Good night."

Mrs. Passmore got up and kissed Zoey on the head as well. "Good night, honey. I love you."

"Good night," she murmured as her mom left the kitchen. She glanced out the window at the Cabral house, silhouetted against the night sky. The house was dark. Lucas must have gone to sleep early. She could picture him in bed, breathing softly, his unruly blond hair spread across the pillow.

For a while that night, before her parents had arrived, Zoey had considered that maybe God was punishing her for fooling around with Aaron Mendel. What other explanation could there be for a day like the one she'd had? But now she realized that her dad was right. None of what had happened really had anything to do with her.

She was just being self-centered.

BENJAMIN

People probably think I have a lot of
secrets. I know a lot of people think of
me as a very private, sometimes cold
person who doesn't like to reveal
what's really going on inside his head.
That's partially true, of course. But I
don't have a lot of deep, dark secrets.
Only one.

I'm scared of regaining my vision.
And I don't mean that I'm scared
of the surgery or the tests or anything like that. I actually have a lot
of faith in doctors. Maybe being blind
makes you more trusting of people
who are there to help you; I'm not
sure.

I'm scared of seeing.

It sounds crazy, but it's true. The
funny thing is, I know I want to see
again—probably as much as I want
anything. But I also want to be able to
appreciate music in the same intense,
all-encompassing way, to hear sounds
that nobody else notices, and to take
immense, sensual pleasure in the scent
of someone I love. In other words, I

want everything in my life to stay the same.

Unfortunately, I don't think that's possible.

Thirteen

"You're doing fine, son," the doctor said. "We'll be done in just a few minutes."

Benjamin nodded. He was lying on a hard, flat cushion—presumably an examination table. The doctor, whose name was Dr. Martin, had been examining him for the past hour. Every now and then he felt faint pressure on his forehead, followed by gloved fingers lifting his eyelids; then he heard Dr. Martin scribbling on a piece of paper. The room was cold and smelled antiseptic.

"Can you move your head a little to the left?" Dr. Martin's deep, rumbling voice was now very close to his ear. "Good. Now open your eyes wide."

"I'll try," Benjamin said. It was difficult for him to keep his eyes open wide for very long—mostly because he'd hardly slept.

"Tired, son?"

"A little," he admitted.

"That's understandable." He laughed sympathetically. "You must have been pretty keyed up."

"Yeah." He'd been pretty keyed up, all right—but not because of the tests. He'd been keyed up because he'd spent the entire night in bed with Nina and nothing had happened.

He still couldn't figure out why. Not that he was mad or frustrated or anything—just a little perplexed. Well, maybe a *little* frustrated. After all, the ride had been very romantic. They'd kissed and held hands pretty much the entire time. And when they'd finally checked into the Malibu Hotel (Nina's choice; she wanted a "tropical atmosphere") under the names of Mr. and Mrs. LaToya Jackson (Nina's choice again) and climbed into a huge, queen-size double bed at around one A.M. . . . well, everything had seemed perfect.

Except Nina had immediately rolled to one side of the huge mattress and cowered there without saying a word. She'd probably fallen asleep after ten minutes.

So Benjamin had lain perfectly still the whole night, pretending to be asleep as well.

Hospital waiting rooms were even worse than buses, Nina decided. For one thing, the fluorescent light exaggerated everyone's facial imperfections. Everyone looked unhealthy, not just the patients. A zit looked like a bright red cancerous mole under those lights. And it *smelled* like sickness, but she couldn't tell if that was the cafeteria. To top it all off, there were about four million magazines—they were either *People* or *House and Garden*, and all of them were at least three years old.

Her stomach grumbled, reminding her of her new resolution to lose weight.

She snatched an issue of *People* off the table. The cover featured a big picture of Bruce and Demi.

"Sudden Split," read the headline. Reading up on celebrity marital problems would kill a few minutes. She wondered suddenly if she and Benjamin would have marital problems. If the previous night was an indication of things to come, they might as well set up an appointment with the marriage counselor now.

It didn't make sense. Everything had been going great until they'd gotten into bed. Then Benjamin had fallen asleep in about fifteen seconds flat. True, she'd been a little nervous. She'd been reluctant to make the first move. But he'd been completely dead to the world. There might as well have been a sign over the door that read, Abandon Libido, All Ye Who Enter Here.

Nina tossed the magazine aside. If she and Benjamin were headed for Bruce-and-Demi land, she didn't want to know about it.

"Just one last little look and we'll be all done here," Dr. Martin said.

Benjamin was hardly listening. The more he thought about it, the more guilty he felt. They'd never actually discussed sleeping together. Maybe Nina wasn't ready to go all the way yet. After all, she was still coming to terms with what her slimebag uncle had done to her. That guy was rotting away in a Minnesota jail, but the effects of abuse never went away; Benjamin knew that.

Still, Nina had been giving him signals, hadn't she? Or maybe she hadn't. It was far more likely that since *he* had been thinking about sex so much, he'd interpreted everything she said as a signal. Besides, it wasn't as if they would have had sex the previous night, anyway. He hadn't even thought about condoms. Sex had been the last thing on his mind—well not the *last*, but certainly not the first—when he'd been packing. Now that he was in Boston, how would he even go about getting them? He couldn't just walk into a store, because Nina would be there with him.

"Don't fall asleep on me, son," Dr. Martin said. "We're almost there."

"Don't worry," Benjamin grumbled. "I'm too keyed up."

IF YOU'RE NOT READY
TO USE CONDOMS,
YOU'RE NOT READY
TO HAVE SEX.

Nina had noticed the sign when she'd first walked past the nurses' station, but now it caught her eye again. It was hanging above a cigarette machine, which struck her as a pretty odd place for it. Maybe hospitals liked to confine all potentially hazardous vices to one small area.

Wait a second.

Hospitals didn't have cigarette machines.

Nina stood and began walking toward it. As she approached, she could see that whatever the thing was, it was definitely *not* a cigarette machine. The shape was wrong, and it was too colorful. She squinted. It looked like a gum-ball machine, or a . . .

All of a sudden she turned bright red.

It was a condom dispenser.

She glanced around surreptitiously to see if anyone was staring at her, then leaned forward to get a close look. There were rows and rows and rows of brightly colored packets on display. Lubricated. Nonlubricated. Ribbed. Reservoir-tipped. Nina bit her tongue, fighting the urge to laugh. It was a pretty impressive array. She hadn't realized there were so many options.

Her eyes flashed to a sign near the money slot: Condoms Greatly Reduce the Risk of Unwanted Pregnancy and/or Sexually Transmitted Disease, such as HIV/AIDS and Hepatitis B.

Well. She certainly didn't want to get pregnant. And she didn't want to contract any diseases, either—although she was pretty sure that Benjamin had been with only one other person, that being Claire, the High Priestess of Satan and her older sister.

And she wasn't sure *who* Claire had been with.

"Well, that's it," Dr. Martin announced. "Good news, Benjamin. Everything I've seen here today indicates that you're the perfect candidate."

Benjamin smiled, feeling a surge of excitement. He'd successfully jumped the first hurdle. All that was left now was the surgery itself.

"Do you have any questions for me before we call your parents in?"

"Uh . . . my parents aren't here," Benjamin said. "They, ah, couldn't make it. You see, they run a restaurant, and they couldn't get away."

"I see." Dr. Martin paused for a minute. "So who brought you here?"

"My girlfriend."

"Your girlfriend. Do you have any questions before I bring your girlfriend in here to take you home?"

"Actually, I do." He cleared his throat. The question he wanted to ask Dr. Martin wasn't about the surgery, but this was a hospital, right? And this was certainly a health-related issue. "Do you know . . . do you know where I can get some condoms?"

Nina paced back and forth in front of the machine several times. *If you're not ready to use condoms, you're not ready to have sex.* Well, she was pretty sure she was ready. For both. She'd been telling herself on the bus that she was ready, long before she'd seen this sign. Maybe the sign was an omen. Maybe it was the Supreme Being's way of decreeing that yes, Nina Geiger truly *was* ready to lose her virginity.

Sure, she had a few lingering doubts and fears—but she knew she loved Benjamin. She knew she'd probably want to be with him forever. This would be the perfect way to seal their relationship.

The only problem was putting the money in the machine and actually *buying* the condoms—in front of the entire hospital waiting room. It wasn't quite the same as buying a pack of Lucky Strikes.

"Condoms?" Dr. Martin asked. "According to what you told the nurse over the phone on Wednesday, you're not sexually active."

"I'm *not*," Benjamin said awkwardly. "At least, I haven't been yet. But, ah . . ."

"You want to amend that situation," Dr. Martin finished.

"Something like that," Benjamin mumbled, suddenly feeling extremely stupid.

"Well, I'll start by saying it's not a doctor's place to judge his patients. So I'm not going to tell you what's right or wrong. I'm just going to present you with some facts. Fair enough?"

"Fair enough," Benjamin replied.

"First of all, do you know how to apply a condom?"

Benjamin knew he was bright red. "Well . . . I mean . . . I never have. . . ."

"If you do decide to have sex, you must have your partner read you the instructions on the packet—and you must follow those instructions carefully and exactly. Even applied correctly, a condom is only eighty-five percent effective as a contraceptive."

For some reason Dr. Martin's dull, matter-of-fact tone only made Benjamin even more embarrassed. He fidgeted on the table, wishing he could just roll off and hide underneath it. He should have never opened his big mouth.

"Second, a condom is by no means a hundred percent effective in preventing the spread of STDs—sexually transmitted diseases. That's a myth many young people accept as fact."

"Well . . . uh . . . we don't have to worry about that."

"I see. Why? Are you from another planet?"

Benjamin groaned inwardly. "Neither of us has ever had sex before."

"You know this for a fact?"

"I'm positive."

"You trust your girlfriend, and that's good. Trust is in short demand these days."

"I *trust* my girlfriend," Benjamin said firmly.

"And I'm not saying you shouldn't. It's wonderful to be in a loving, trusting relationship." Dr. Martin sighed. "These are just important things to consider. And now you have the facts. As I said, the decision is yours."

Benjamin sat up straight. "I've already made my decision."

"Fine. Now that our little chat about safe sex is over, do you have any questions about the surgery?"

What is your problem? Take the money out of your pocket and put it in the machine!

Nina fumbled for her wallet with moist, trembling hands. If nobody had noticed her before, people were now probably starting to wonder. A girl with purple lipstick and army fatigues pacing and muttering to herself in front of a condom machine wasn't all that easy to ignore.

"Nina Geiger?" a deep voice called.

Nina whipped around. A tall, bearded African-American doctor was standing in the doorway at the other end of the waiting room.

"That's me," she answered.

"You can come in now," he said, gesturing.

Nina crammed her wallet back in her pocket. The doctor held the door open as she marched back down the hall. Well, that's what she got for being such a wuss. Thanks to all that debate and anxiety, she'd managed to avoid making any decision at all. So much for a beautiful night at the Malibu Hotel.

The doctor led her to a small examination room. Benjamin was sitting on the table. She was taken aback momentarily by the sight of Benjamin without his dark glasses. His eyes were unfocused, but in the bright light, she noticed for the first time in a long while what a deep, gorgeous brown they were.

"Hey," she said, squeezing his hand. "How'd it go?"

"Great, I guess." He smiled and shifted his eyes

to the doctor. "Dr. Martin here thinks I'm good to go, right?"

The doctor nodded. "That's right. And if it's okay with you and you parents, I'd like to proceed quickly. Maybe even in the next two weeks or so."

Nina threw her arms around Benjamin's neck. "I'm so happy for you," she whispered.

"I'm happy for me, too," he said.

Dr. Martin handed Benjamin his dark glasses and helped him off the table. "Please notify your parents about this as soon as possible. Benjamin. I'll want to talk to them in the next few days. You'll also have to fill out some forms at the nurses' station."

Benjamin extended his hand. "Thank you so much, Dr. Martin," he said as the doctor shook it. "For *everything*."

For the first time since Nina had been in his presence, Dr. Martin smiled. It was a warm, wise sort of smile that instantly made Nina feel that Benjamin was in excellent hands.

"It's my pleasure," Dr. Martin replied. His face grew serious again. "And Nina, I'm going to tell you what I told Benjamin. I noticed you were standing by the condom dispenser. If you two have indeed made the decision to become sexually active, you must make sure Benjamin follows the instructions for applying the condom *exactly* as given on the packet."

Fourteen

Zoey was conscious of a sound. It was a thumping or knocking—growing louder and louder.

"Zoey?" a boy's muffled voice called. "Are you up?"

Slowly Zoey opened her eyes. She was in bed. Bright sunlight was streaming through her curtains. Someone was knocking on her bedroom door. "Hello?" she croaked, propping herself on her elbows.

"It's Lucas. Can I come in?"

"Uh, sure," she said, feeling slightly confused. The door opened, but Lucas didn't step in. "What time is it?" she asked hoarsely.

"A little past one." Lucas stood hesitantly in the doorway, looking at the ground. He still had his coat on, and his blond hair was plastered to his head, as if he'd only just taken off his hat. "I've been—ah— waiting downstairs for a while, but your parents wanted to let you sleep."

"I guess I must have been pretty tired." The memory of everything that had happened the day before were flooding back now, and with it, waves of guilt. She glanced at Lucas. Usually when he was in her room, he couldn't take his eyes off her. Now he was deliberately looking away. He was staring at the floor as if it were about to reveal the secrets of the universe.

"I guess so," he said quietly.

"Lucas, I'm sorry about the way I've been acting," she blurted.

He looked up and tried to smile, but he couldn't quite manage it. "Yeah, well, I've been doing some thinking."

"Some thinking?" she repeated.

"Yeah."

"What kind of thinking?" she asked, frightened by the grim tone of his voice.

He took a deep breath and closed the door behind him, then looked her in the eye. "I was thinking that maybe we could use some time apart, you know?"

"Some time apart?" she repeated blankly. "Why?"

"Come on, Zo." He laughed hopelessly. "How do you think I feel right now? First you blew me off all day at school. You won't tell me what's bothering you. You lied about not getting my note. . . ."

Zoey blinked. How did he know about that?

"Zoey, I know you always go to your locker before gym," he said, as if reading her thoughts. "That's why I left it there. I'm not as stupid as you think."

"I don't think you're stupid," she whispered.

"Well, anyway, you lied about that. Then you acted like going to the mall with me was torture." His voice hardened. "You treated me like crap, Zo. And *then*, when you found out about Benjamin, you didn't even think to call me later. These aren't the signs of a healthy relationship, are they?"

"Lucas—I love you."

He shook his head. "Yeah. Well, if this is love, I think I'm gonna check into a monastery."

"What do you want me to do?" she pleaded. Her eyes were starting to mist over. "Just tell me."

"I'm telling you. I don't want you to do anything. I think maybe we should just take a break for a while."

"You mean *break up*?" she cried.

He shrugged.

"Lucas . . ." She leaped out of bed, not caring that she was wearing only underwear and an oversized T-shirt. The floor felt like ice against her bare feet. "Please—let's just talk." She put her hands on his arms, trying to meet his gaze, but he kept looking away. "I know I acted like a total bitch yesterday, believe me, but—"

"*Bitch* is an understatement."

She paused. Why hadn't she seen this coming? Had she been so swept up in Aaron that she hadn't even noticed that Lucas might have been losing interest? Somehow the notion of Lucas's just breaking up with her—just like that—had never crossed her mind. "I need you, Lucas," she choked out. "That's . . . that's all I have to say."

Lucas put a finger on her face and brushed away a lone tear. "If you need me, then why do you keep pushing me away?" he asked softly. "What makes you think I don't need *you*?"

"Do you need me?" she whispered.

He reached out and gently pulled her against him. "Of course I do," he said. "Why do you think I'm here trying so hard to break up with you?"

Zoey smiled. She closed her eyes, listening to his

heartbeat through his chest. "I don't want to break up."

"Well, I don't want to, either," he said. "But things have to change."

"I know," she said. "They will. I promise."

Lucas laughed.

"What is it?" she asked.

"Oh, I was just thinking about how I had my mind all made up to break up with you—until I was in the same room with you for about thirty seconds."

There was a knock on the door. Zoey and Lucas instantly sprang apart. "Who is it?" she asked.

"Lara."

Lara! Lucas made a face—but Zoey was instantly thrown into a panic. She threw the door open. "Come in, come in," she whispered, dragging her inside. "Have you seen Mom and Dad yet today?"

Lara nodded. "Yeah—but Jake got to me first. He stopped by at about six A.M. and . . . uh . . . explained the situation."

"Oh." Zoey couldn't help noticing how terrible Lara looked. Her face was pale and swollen, and her eyes were so puffy that she could hardly open them. "Well, that's good."

Lara glanced at Lucas, who was looking very confused, then back at Zoey. "I guess, uh . . . I guess I owe you some thanks."

"Don't worry about it. Just make sure it never happens again."

She nodded somberly. "Look—sorry to barge in on you like this. I just wanted to say thanks." She closed the door behind her.

"What was *that* all about?" Lucas asked.

Zoey shook her head. "Lara got bombed by herself

last night. Luckily she called Jake. He came over and put her to bed—and then told me to tell my mom and dad that she was sick.'' She wrinkled her brow. ''She's out of control.''

''Are, uh . . .'' Lucas licked his lips. ''Are she and Jake . . . ?''

Zoey shrugged. ''It sure seems that way. But you'd have to ask him, I guess.''

''Jeez.'' Lucas laughed. ''There's never a dull moment at the Passmore house these days, is there? Which reminds me, Benjamin called about twenty minutes ago.''

''Is he okay?''

Lucas nodded. ''I guess all the tests went really well. He's gonna explain everything when he gets back tomorrow. Your mom said he sounded nervous but happy.''

''Well, *that's* good.'' Zoey rubbed her face. Her skin was still moist from crying. ''Whew. You're right. It never is dull around here, is it?''

''I guess not.'' Lucas looked at her. ''You want to get back in bed? By yourself, I mean,'' he added quickly.

She smirked. ''No, no, that's all right. I'm wide awake now. You know what? I have an idea.''

''What's that?''

''Let's go to Weymouth today. Let's go back to the mall and pretend that the past few days never happened. Let's just start over. Blank slate. How does that sound?''

Lucas leaned forward and kissed her. ''Sounds perfect. I'll wait downstairs.''

For a moment, as Zoey listened to Lucas's boots clomping loudly on the staircase, she felt another wave of guilt. He would never know just how desperately she wanted to pretend that the last few days had never happened.

Even as she stood at the front door of the Grays' B&B, Claire still wasn't sure she'd go through with her plan. Even *she* had to admit that snooping around behind someone's back was pretty low. Then again, she'd done some low things in the past, and she'd learned that the ends frequently justified the means.

Besides, her visit looked very innocent. She was just dropping off a book for Aaron—*The Greenhouse Effect: Global Warming and Its Consequences*. Just some light reading, she thought with a wry smile. With it she'd enclosed a note that read, *If I'd known you were so interested in climatology, I'd have given you this book sooner. Weather isn't all just rainbows and snowflakes, you know. It can be a very provocative subject.*

She looked up at Aaron's dark window and thought, *That'll teach you to play dinner games with me, Aaron Mendel.*

The freezing wind up on the ridge had begun to make her hands sting, demanding that she make a decision. She rang the doorbell. Maybe dropping this book off didn't look all that innocent, but at least it looked better than what she really had in mind.

Kalif, Aisha's little brother, opened the door. "Hi, Claire," he said.

"Hi, Kalif." She smiled. "Is Eesh here?" she asked, knowing full well Aisha was in Weymouth with Christopher.

"Nope," he replied.

"Oh. Well, do you know if Aaron Mendel is

here?'' she asked, knowing full well he was in Weymouth with Sarah and Mr. Geiger.

''I don't know. You can take a look if you want.''

''Thanks.'' Claire stepped inside. ''I just wanted to
drop off this book for him.''

Kalif shrugged. ''Go ahead. His room is upstairs,
around the corner to the left.'' He disappeared into
the residence part of the bed-and-breakfast, where he
and the rest of the Grays lived.

''Thanks,'' Claire called, heading for the stairs.
That had been easy enough.

She slowed as she rounded the corner and headed
down the narrow little hall to his room. The door was
closed. She could just drop the book off outside and
leave. Nothing was forcing her to enter his room. For
all she knew, he'd locked his door. There was no
harm in checking.

The doorknob turned, and the door swung open.

Okay, she was inside, but she didn't have to stay.

Her eyes roamed the small, cozy room. The four-
poster bed was unmade. Aaron's guitar stood propped
against the wall in the corner. Clothes were strewn
across the floor. *Why is it that all boys are slobs*? she
wondered.

A small trunk jutting out from under his bed caught
her attention. It seemed odd that he would have
brought a trunk to Chatham Island, considering he'd
originally planned to stay for only a few days. Maybe
his father had shipped it to him when his plans had
changed.

Claire knelt beside it and gingerly pulled it out
from under the bed. The lock was hanging loose. She
swung the lid open so that it rested against the bed.
There wasn't much to look at inside: CDs, books,

tapes, packs of guitar strings, and a shoe box.

Maybe the shoebox held some surprises.

She lifted it from the trunk and placed it on the floor, tossing the cover aside. A smile broke out on her face. *Always trust your instincts, Claire,* she congratulated herself.

The shoebox was filled with letters.

She picked one off the top: a single page of pink stationery.

July 23

Dear Aaron,

I'm just writing to say hi. I don't know why I believed you when you told me that we would keep in touch all summer. I guess I was just hoping.

I've been thinking about you a lot. I know we were only together that one night and we were both pretty trashed, but it was nice. I don't know if you know this, but it was my first time.

Now I'm sure I've totally freaked you out and you think I'm some Fatal Attraction-*type psycho who's going to come after you and kill all your pets. Don't worry. I mean, it was great, but it wasn't that great. No offense.*

Oh, boy. As you can imagine, this letter isn't quite turning out the way I'd planned. But I think I'm going to send it anyway. I hope you're having a great summer, and I'd love to hear from you.

Love,

Kate

Claire carefully folded the letter and put it back in the box. She sneered. It was amazing how revealing four short paragraphs could be. In less than a minute, she'd learned that Aaron was a drinker, he wasn't a virgin, and he liked to take advantage of willing girls. Interesting. What other little gems lurked in that cardboard treasure chest?

She peered into the box. There must have been another twenty-five letters in there—at least. Nevertheless, she fought the temptation to look at any more. It was wrong; she knew it was wrong. Besides, she'd found what she'd been looking for, and it had far exceeded her expectations.

As she replaced the lid and delicately placed the shoe box back in the trunk, she wondered why Aaron would keep a letter like that. Was it some kind of trophy? She could imagine him saying to himself, *Here's another girl I banged—chalk that one up for the old shoe box.* Claire had heard enough grisly stories about serial killers keeping snapshots of their victims to recognize a lesser variation on the same twisted theme. Then again, maybe he'd kept it because he really liked the girl and had written her back. Doubtful—but possible.

She closed the trunk and shoved it back under the bed. Suddenly she frowned.

Who was she to judge Aaron so harshly on such little evidence?

She was the one poking around his room. So he got drunk every now and then and had sex—big deal. Her own ex-boyfriend wasn't any better. Jake had done the same thing with Louise Kronenberger—only he'd gotten so drunk, he couldn't even *remember* the sex part.

No, the difference between Aaron and Jake was that Aaron was intelligent and manipulative. He didn't get caught. He did what he had to do to get what he wanted.

And he was very sexy.

In fact, Claire realized, she was still very attracted to him in spite of what she'd discovered. Maybe, in an odd way, even more so.

She stood up and left the room, closing the door behind her. Coming here had certainly constituted a weird little episode in her life. It wasn't the sort of thing she would ever want to repeat. But she paused for a moment and smiled, wondering briefly what Kate looked like. For some reason Claire pictured her looking like Nina. Maybe it was that line about the *"Fatal Attraction*-type psycho."

Nina

Well, it happened. The Deed occurred sometime after one a.m. on Sunday, December 8, in room 428 of the not-so-elegant Malibu Hotel in downtown Boston. Ooh, it's just like a fairy tale, isn't it? (That's a joke. Ha, ha.) And all this in spite of Dr. Martin's heroic efforts to make us feel like the two biggest butt-munches on the planet. It's too bad America's Funniest Home Videos wasn't there— in the hospital, I mean. That moment definitely would have qualified for the big season finale.

But I'm not mad. On the contrary, I feel I should thank the good doctor. With one concise, clinical instruction regarding said Deed, he opened our hearts and souls and innermost desires to each other. Yep— there wasn't much gray area left after Dr. Martin opened his mouth. It was pretty clear both Benjamin and I had a hankering to "do the nasty."

Which reminds me: I really should find out where that phrase originated. It doesn't make any sense. Nasty is not a word that leaps to mind.

I guess all I can say now is that I'm more in love with Benjamin than ever before. And not only because I discovered he never did sleep with Claire.

BENJAMIN

I swear I was ready to kill Dr. Martin. I'm glad I didn't. Killing him wouldn't have been too smart, considering that he's the one who has to perform the surgery. However, I can safely say that never in my entire life have I felt like such a complete imbecile.

Miraculously, everything worked out for the best—after some initial awkwardness, of course. But once each of us knew what was on the other's mind, we were able to talk. We talked about everything—our feelings, the future, Claire (who Nina thought I slept with, for some unfathomable reason), safe sex (Dr. Martin would have been proud)—even Nina's uncle. To quote a frequently abused cliché, "We laughed and we cried."

And then we retired to room 428 of the Malibu Hotel.

Fifteen

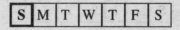

On Sunday, Benjamin and Nina returned to Chatham Island. They were met at the ferry landing by the entire Passmore family, including Lara. Mr. and Mrs. Passmore then treated everyone to dinner at the restaurant. Benjamin apologized profusely for having run away. Mr. Passmore forgave him and added that if Benjamin ever tried to pull a stunt like that again, he would break both his legs.

After dinner Nina returned home, told her father that the Philharmonic had been an experience she'd never forget, and immediately fell asleep.

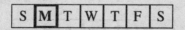

On Monday, Aaron stopped by the Geigers' to thank Claire for the book. Claire suggested that they watch the moonrise on her widow's walk. Aaron agreed, but once they were up on the roof, he began asking questions about Claire's friends, especially Zoey. Claire decided it was too cold to watch the moonrise. On her way down the ladder, she told Aaron that she thought Zoey and Lucas would be the first of her friends to get married.

Nina called Zoey to ask what had been bothering her all her last week. Zoey told her that Lara had been getting on her nerves but that things were much better now.

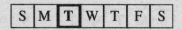

On Tuesday, Zoey went to Aisha's ostensibly to get help with her math homework. On her way out, she slipped a note under Aaron's door explaining in a very apologetic manner that kissing him had been wonderful, but that they couldn't see each other anymore.

After enduring a dinner with both the Mendels, Nina escaped to her room. Claire barged in and asked if anything exciting had happened on her trip. Nina told Claire that it was none of her business—and then asked Claire if she was a virgin. Claire told Nina that whether or not she was a virgin was none of Nina's business, then left. Nina was sure that Claire's agitation implied she wasn't.

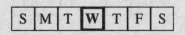

On Wednesday, Christopher sold his island car to Sarah Mendel for three hundred dollars cash. He then

144

boarded the 11:10 ferry, went straight to a Weymouth pawnshop, and spent the entire sum on an antique silver ring. Later he called Aisha and made plans for dinner Saturday night at La Cocina Della Fontana, a fancy Italian restaurant in Portside. Aisha asked what the big occasion was, but Christopher said it was a surprise.

When Nina got home from school and learned that Sarah Mendel had bought an island car, she immediately called Zoey. Nina was sure this meant Sarah intended on staying for good. Zoey agreed; it was a clear sign that Sarah and Mr. Geiger were planning to get married. Nina said she was contemplating moving to another state.

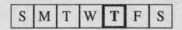

S	M	T	W	T	F	S

On Thursday, Lucas came home with Zoey after school and suggested, not so subtly, that they do more than just make out. Zoey got angry and told him to drop it. Lucas got angry and brought up the fact that she still hadn't told him what had been bothering her the week before. Zoey told Lucas to go home, and he obliged by storming out of the house without saying good-bye.

Downstairs, Nina was reading Benjamin *The Snows of Kilimanjaro*, by Ernest Hemingway, when Benjamin got a call from Boston General. Dr. Martin told him that the surgery was scheduled for Friday, December 27, and that Benjamin would probably have to remain in the hospital through New Year's Day.

S	M	T	W	T	**F**	S

On Friday, Jake went straight to the Passmores' after school and spent the entire evening with Lara. After Lara fell asleep, Jake quietly searched the room. He found a bottle of vodka and two bottles of tequila, all of which he confiscated.

Nina also went straight to the Passmores' after school. She'd planned on spending some time alone with Benjamin, but since Zoey and Lucas were in a fight, Zoey ended up spending the entire evening with them, giving new meaning to the phrases "fifth wheel" and "three's a crowd."

Sixteen

Zoey stumbled into the kitchen a little past eleven o'clock on Saturday morning. A light snow was falling, and the backyard was already blanketed with a thin, patchy white cover. Her gaze wandered up the hill to Lucas's house. She was half hoping he'd be out on his deck, looking down at her—but he wasn't.

She sank down into a seat at the table. They hadn't even spoken since Thursday night. All through history and French on Friday, they'd sat next to each other without so much as a single hello. And then when school was over, Lucas had deliberately taken a later ferry home. She shook her head. They were giving each other the silent treatment. What a mature way to handle their problems. They might as well be in kindergarten.

Well, if he wanted to go on acting like a jerk, fine. *He* was wrong. The whole situation was pretty amazing, really. He just couldn't seem to get it through his thick skull that she wasn't ready to sleep with him yet. What would it take to convince him—a chastity belt?

Maybe he'd had the right idea when he suggested that they needed some time apart to think things over.

Not an official breakup—just a little time off. A kind of trial separation. She was pretty sure she wanted to keep going out with him. But maybe if he saw how miserable his life would be without her, he would start thinking twice before his horniness got the best of him.

Yes, she *did* want to keep going out with him. She knew that. And as long as she could continue to stay clear of Aaron Mendel, she wouldn't be in any danger of thinking otherwise.

Benjamin walked into the kitchen wearing nothing but a bathrobe and his dark glasses. "Trying to communicate telepathically with Lucas?" he asked.

Zoey turned from the window. "And what makes you think I was even looking at his house?" she asked, trying unsuccessfully to sound surprised.

Benjamin opened the refrigerator door and began running his hands over the containers of food inside. "Because when you're in here, not eating or making any noise, I know you're looking up at your boyfriend's house." He grinned. "Even a blind person knows these things, Zo."

Zoey stuck her tongue out at him. That was one thing a blind person wouldn't notice, at least. "You're just feeling all warm and fuzzy inside because you and your girlfriend are like Lucy and Ricky Ricardo. Without the laugh track, that is."

"Oh, Lu-cee, I'm ho-o-ome," he called, in a dead-on impersonation of Desi Arnaz. He held up his finger. "Wait. You're right. There really *isn't* a laugh track here." His mouth dropped open. "Oh, no!"

"Maybe we should get Dad to install one," Zoey mumbled. "This house is starting to remind me of a bad TV sitcom."

"Yeah—kind of like a zanier, wackier version of *Mork and Mindy*, only not in Denver." He pulled a bottle of orange juice from the refrigerator and placed it on the table.

"Exactly. You're Robin Williams, and Nina is Pam Dawber."

"Pam Dawber? I can't believe you know her name." Benjamin shook his head. "You watch *way* too much TV, Zo. Anyway, you're wrong about Nina and me. We're not like that at all. We have our problems. Take last night, for instance. I really wanted to be alone with her, but she insisted that we keep her best friend company, because her best friend was feeling really mopey about her boyfriend. It was totally lame. More like *Three's Company* than *Mork and Mindy*."

"You're a laugh a minute, Benjamin," Zoey said dully. "Stop it. You're killing me."

Benjamin shrugged. "I aim to please."

"Hi, guys," Lara sang out, strolling into the kitchen.

Zoey grinned for a moment. Once again Lara was wearing her polka-dot pajamas. Even if Lara lived with the Passmores for the rest of her life, Zoey doubted she'd ever get used to those pajamas.

"Hey, Lara," Benjamin said. "Sleep well?"

"Like a baby," Lara said, grabbing a glass and helping herself to juice. "Hey—was that you imitating Ricky Ricardo? That was pretty good."

Benjamin struck a cocky pose. "If you think that's good, you should hear my Homer Simpson."

"I'd rather not," Zoey muttered under her breath.

"It makes sense, you know," Lara said after she'd

noisily gulped down her entire glass. She nodded, looking preoccupied. "I mean, that you'd be so good at doing imitations."

Zoey shot her a look. What was that supposed to mean? But Lara just kept looking at Benjamin, oblivious to the tension that had suddenly enveloped the room.

Benjamin hesitated for the merest fraction of a second, then said, "Yeah. Blind people make great ventriloquists, too."

"They do?" Lara asked curiously. "What's a ventriloquist?"

"One of those people who talks to a wooden dummy. They kind of died out in the seventies." He grinned at Zoey. "Just like *Mork and Mindy*."

Lara raised her eyebrows. "Man, you guys are weird."

"That's another thing about blind people," Benjamin said, but the humor had gone out of his voice. "They're weird."

Lara shrugged and put her glass in the sink. "I guess so."

"What is it with you?" Zoey snapped. "Do you always insult people first thing in the morning?"

Benjamin shook his head miserably. "Zoey . . ."

"Hey, I wasn't insulting anyone," Lara said. She glanced at the two of them, then left the kitchen. "Sorry if you took it that way," she called.

"What is her problem?" Zoey whispered, enraged.

Benjamin sighed and sat down beside her. "Don't worry about it, Zo. I couldn't care less. She's had a rough time of it. She's not exactly a people person, you know?"

"Benjamin, come on! How can you just—"

"Getting angry isn't gonna do anyone any good."

"Oh, *please*," Zoey groaned. "You sound like Dad."

Benjamin smiled halfheartedly. "Maybe I do. But think about it. She's living here now, and she isn't going anywhere soon. It's a situation, and we have to deal with it."

Zoey put her face in her hands. "I think you had the right idea by running away."

"That's definitely *not* the right idea." He laughed. "Forget about it, all right?"

"Fine," Zoey said. She looked up. "So anyway, what were we just talking about?"

"Bad sitcoms. Speaking of which, don't you think that calling Lucas would be more effective than staring at his house?"

Lucas was very glad his parents had gone to Weymouth to buy a Christmas tree. Well, he wasn't thrilled about the Christmas tree part, but he was glad to be alone. Christmas was a lame holiday as far as he was concerned. It was one of the things he *hadn't* missed while he'd been locked up in Youth Authority.

He paced around his room, feeling antsy. The night before, he'd decided to stay at home all day and get a start on studying for exams. It wasn't as if he had any big plans or anything. He and Zoey weren't even speaking anymore. But he had to admit that doing homework on a Saturday didn't hold much appeal.

The phone rang. Lucas jumped, feeling momentarily excited, then angry. If Zoey was calling, he didn't want to talk to her. *She* was at fault here. He raced down the stairs and into the living room, where he stood in front of the answering machine. After two more rings, the machine clicked.

"You've reached the Cabral residence," his father's colorless voice announced. *"Please leave a message, and one of the Cabrals will get back to you as soon as possible."*

There was a beep. "Hi, Lucas. It's me."

Lucas clenched his fists. Zoey, of course. He couldn't help but feel a minor degree of relief—which made him even angrier.

"Uh . . . I don't know if you're home or not, but I just wanted to talk. I think it's stupid for us not to talk, don't you? Anyway, when you get this message, give me a call. I'll be home all day." The machine clicked again.

Maybe it was stupid that they weren't talking, but he wasn't going to call her back. Not yet, at least. Not until she called and left a message that was much more apologetic—one that specifically said she was sorry.

Then, *maybe*, he would call her back.

Benjamin counted the last few steps down Lighthouse Road to the Geigers' house. Even in a snowstorm, the walk was second nature; he could navigate the roads of North Harbor as well as any sighted person.

In a few weeks, of course, he might never have to count the steps again.

He kicked at the snow. He'd promised himself he wasn't going to think about the operation anymore. He couldn't afford to be distracted, what with exams coming up—and he didn't want to ask for any extensions or postponements. He didn't want any sympathy. He just wanted to do his work, then go to Boston when the time came.

If only Lara hadn't opened her big mouth.

Zoey was right. That girl *did* have a problem. She was probably the most vulgar, tactless person Benjamin had ever met. It would be worth getting his sight back if only to keep Lara from making any more idiotic and offensive comments about blind people.

He marched up onto the Geigers' covered porch, glad to be out of the snow, and rang the doorbell. The muffled sound of some punk rock band came from deep within the house. Nina. A moment later he heard slow, deliberate steps in the stairwell. Claire. He smiled. It was still a small, secret point of pride with him that he could tell people apart by the way they approached a door. Nina always bounded down the steps eagerly, as if she were expecting a surprise. Claire, on the other hand, never hurried. For anyone.

The door opened. "Hey, Claire," he said.

"You still know when it's me," she said. "I'm touched. Come in, come in."

"I doubt I'll forget anytime soon." He wiped his feet and stepped inside.

"Hello, Benjamin!" Mr. Geiger called cheerily from the kitchen. "Happy holidays!"

"Hi, Mr. Geiger. Uh . . . happy holidays to you, too."

"Don't ask," Claire whispered, closing the door. "He hasn't been himself lately."

"Ms. Mendel?" Benjamin whispered back.

"That's right. The midget. For some reason, she has the same effect on him as Prozac does."

He grinned. "That sounds like something your sister would say."

"Well, I guess for once we actually agree on something. Speaking of Nina, you can probably tell from the melodious chain saw sounds we're enjoying right now that she's in her room." She touched his arm lightly. "You really have to start working on her taste in music."

"This is *music?*" he asked sarcastically, following her up the stairs.

"According to Nina. But who understands kids today? I'll see you later, Benjamin." She continued up the next set of stairs to her room, which was on the third floor.

"Bye, Claire." He paused, struck by the thought of how only a few short months earlier, he would have followed Claire right up to her room. He shook his head. Breaking up with her was probably one of the best decisions he'd ever made. And he was thankful their present relationship had assumed some degree of normalcy.

"Nina!" he shouted. He pounded on the door in a vain effort to be heard over the music. "Are you still alive in there?"

The volume faded. "Hold on, hold on!" she called. "Sorry! One sec."

"Hey, I don't care if you're naked or anything," he said quietly. "I'm blind, remember?"

"Very funny." She opened the door and pulled him inside, then began kissing him fervently. After about ten seconds, she stopped.

"Wow." Benjamin took a deep breath. "What was that for?"

"Why? You complaining?"

"No . . ."

"It's just my new way of saying hello to you." She slapped her bed. "Here, come sit."

He sat beside her and felt for her hand. "So what were you listening to, anyway? Madonna?"

"Very funny. They're called Oasis. Maybe you've heard of them?"

"You know how out of touch I am, Nina. All this rock-and-roll stuff is way over my head."

"Well, I guess we shouldn't talk about music, then."

Benjamin squeezed her fingers. "Maybe we should just stop talking altogether," he said slyly. "Snow always gets me in a romantic mood. . . ."

"Wait!" she said, giggling. "Hold your horses, pal. I actually wanted to talk about something with you."

"Oh, yeah? What?"

She cleared her throat. "This is serious."

"Okay," he replied, feeling vaguely apprehensive. "Shoot."

"You know how you said you didn't want anyone to stay with you in Boston any longer than one or two days? After the operation?"

He nodded, swallowing. "Yeah. I don't want anyone to miss New Year's Eve on my account. It would be stupid."

Nina laughed. "Well, I'm defying your command. I'm gonna stay with you the whole time."

"Nina, come on—"

"New Year's Eve is gonna suck without you anyway, Benjamin. I'd rather be with *you* than at some lame party where everyone is chugging champagne and counting down to midnight with Dick Clark."

"You'd rather be sitting in a hospital?" he said in

a flat, biting voice. "Give me a break, Nina."

"Yeah, I would. Why is that so hard for you to believe?"

"Because it's not true," he said sharply. He let her hand go.

"What, are you mad or something now?" she said. Her voice was teasing—and it infuriated him.

"Yeah, I am," he snapped. "Because I don't want your pity. I want you to have fun on New Year's Eve."

"You think I want to stay with you out of *pity?* Is that really what you think?"

"What other reason is there?" he demanded.

"Maybe I enjoy your company more than anyone else's on the planet. Then again, if you're going to act like a total butthead, maybe I should reconsider."

"I want you to reconsider."

Nina stood up from the bed. "Benjamin, what the hell is your problem?" she shouted.

Benjamin ran a hand through his hair. Why were they fighting? They'd just *slept* together; they were supposed to be entering a new, exciting phase of their relationship. "I don't have a problem," he said finally.

"Yeah, you do. You've lost your mind. I don't pity you, Benjamin. I know enough not to feel pity for the Blind Wonder."

"Oh, I get it. So *that's* what you think of me."

"No. That's what you think of yourself."

The words struck Benjamin like a slap in the face. She was absolutely right. He *did* think of himself that way. But that was who he was. In a way, that was all he had.

"Benjamin, I'm going to stay with you because I want to be with my boyfriend. That's *it*. If you don't understand that, you need a shrink a lot more than you need a surgeon."

Seventeen

THEMES OF BETRAYAL IN
THE SCARLET LETTER

BY JAKE McROYAN

IN NATHANIEL HAWTHORNE'S
THE SCARLET LETTER

Jake stared at the computer screen. He was miserable. He'd been stuck on the same line—the first—for the past hour. Six lousy words in an hour; that was an average of one word every ten minutes. At this rate, he figured, he would finish sometime in January. He glanced at his watch. Eight-thirty. Eight-thirty on a Saturday night, no less. He should be out seeing a movie, or at a party, or lying in Lara's bed listening to music—anywhere but in his room doing homework. There was always Sunday. . . .

No. He'd made the decision to stay home, and he was going to stick to it. He needed the discipline. Discipline was good. Discipline kept his life from falling apart, and his life would certainly fall apart if he failed English this semester. Even if he wrote the most brilliant, insightful essay ever, it would only earn him a C; the paper was now over a week late. And Jake knew that barring a minor miracle, he would not be writing the most brilliant, insightful essay ever—not by a long shot.

He cracked his knuckles, glaring at the screen. It was like a workout: a mental workout. He could do this. In the next twenty-four hours, he would crank out a 1,750-word masterpiece.

But before he could even place his fingers on the keyboard again, there was a knock on his sliding glass door.

Jake shook his head. "Just a sec."

Lara walked in and pulled the door shut behind her without saying a word.

"Lara," he began in an apologetic tone, "I told you that I had to write this—"

"You missed one," she interrupted.

Jake frowned. "What do you mean?"

Her face was expressionless. "You missed one," she repeated. She reached into her coat pocket and pulled out a small brown paper bag. Concealed inside it was a bottle—a bottle with an all too familiar shape. "See?"

"Oh, jeez." Jake felt the color draining from his face. "Lara—"

"Who gave you permission to go through my stuff?" she shouted. "Huh, Mr. Goody-Goody, Holier-Than-Thou, Never-Touch-Another-Drop?" She waved the bag menacingly in his face, swishing the booze hidden inside. "What gives *you* the right to do something like *that?*"

"Come on, Lara," he hissed. "Keep your voice down. I was doing it for your own good, and you know it."

"What—are you worried your dad's gonna hear you and find you down here with some alcoholic floozy? 'My son's too good for a tramp like that,'" she said in a deep, mocking voice. "No, that won't do at—"

"Shut up," Jake whispered furiously. "Is that what you think? That I think of you as some alcoholic floozy?"

"Then why are you keeping us a secret?" she demanded.

"I'm *not.* Everyone knows: Zoey, Benjamin, Lucas—"

"They found out, Jake," she spat. "You didn't tell them. You haven't *told* anyone."

Jake's jaw tightened. He couldn't argue that; she was right. "Fine," he said. "Tomorrow I'll go from house to house and tell everyone on Chatham Island that I'm going out with Lara McAvoy. Now give me the bottle." He reached out and tried to grab it, but she jerked her hand away.

"Damn—you're pretty slow for a jock." She smiled wickedly, waving the bottle above his head. "Didn't your father teach you any manners? If you want something, you gotta say please."

160

"I'm not gonna ask you again. Give me the bottle—or I'm gonna take it."

"Why do you want the bottle so bad, Jakie? You thirsty or something? You want a drink?"

"Damn it, Lara!" he barked. "Stop playing these stupid games. You're making me sick."

"*I'm* making *you* sick? Pretty high and mighty for someone who gets his kicks snooping through people's stuff."

Jake sighed. He was too tired to fight anymore. "Fine, Lara. You win. You're right—I was wrong. Take your bottle and get the hell out of here." He swiveled around and forced himself to stare at his computer screen. "Don't bother coming back."

"I'm not gonna let you off that easily, Jake."

"I don't get it, Lara," he said. He whipped around to face her again. "I'm the one who's trying to help you. If you can't see that, then I'm not gonna waste my time anymore."

She lowered her eyes. "I know you're trying to help me. But you were wrong to do what you did."

"What do you want from me?" he asked. "I'm sorry, okay? Sometimes you gotta do something bad for a greater good. But I guess you don't see it that way."

She shook her head. "No—I *do* see it that way. That's why I'm gonna let you help me get rid of this one last bottle."

Jake scowled. "What do you mean, *help* you?"

"You have to pay for your sins. An eye for an eye."

He shook his head disgustedly. "You're not making any sense, Lara."

"Yes, I *am*, Jake. That's why you and me are splitting this bottle right now.'' She tossed the bag to the floor, revealing a smaller flask of the same brand of tequila she'd been drinking the week before.

"You're crazy, Lara," he whispered. His voice was quavering. "There's no way I'm going to split that bottle with you."

"Fine." She shrugged. "Then I'll go home and drink the whole thing myself. Have it your way."

"Is that some kind of threat?"

"No," she replied matter-of-factly. "It's the truth."

"So you're trying to blackmail me into drinking with you? Is that your version of paying for your sins? I—'' He forced himself to soften his voice. "Lara, don't do this," he pleaded. "For the last time, just give me the bottle."

"But don't you see the beauty of it, Jake?" she asked. She smiled suddenly, as if she were in some kind of religious trance. "It's a symbolic act. Together we finish this last bottle and put drinking behind us forever."

He shook his head. "I already have put drinking behind me," he said in a low, sad voice. "And let me tell you something: *Drinking* is not the way to put drinking behind you."

"So you're saying I'm gonna have to finish this by myself?" Lara demanded, shifting on her feet impatiently.

"I'm saying you should throw that bottle away."

"That's not an option."

"Look—why don't you just sit down on my bed, and . . . and . . . let me just turn off my computer, and we'll just hang out for a while, okay?"

"Well . . . okay," she said finally.

Jake's face brightened. "Good."

Lara sat down on his bed. She twisted the cap off the bottle and tossed the cap on the floor near the bag.

"Lara!"

"Jake, you gotta understand where I'm coming from," she said, staring at the bottle as if she were hypnotized. "This is serious. We've both made a lot of mistakes. It's important that we do this." She spoke in a monotone. "Now. Together."

Jake leaped from his chair and knelt in front of her. He was growing desperate. He could smell the liquor now, its putrid, oily odor. "You're not fooling anyone," he said, placing his hands on her knees. "This isn't some big, momentous ritual or anything. This is an excuse to get drunk because you're pissed I threw out all your bottles. That's *all* it is."

"Call it what you will," she said, shrugging. "But right now you've got a choice. You can either split this with me—which will keep me from getting *completely* bombed—or you can let me go and take your chances." She shoved the bottle under his nose. "Sometimes you gotta do something bad for the greater good, Jakie," she whispered. "Remember?"

Jake's eyes flashed from the bottle to Lara's face, then back again. The bottle wasn't *that* big. She was telling the truth when she said she wouldn't get all that drunk. *Neither* of them would get that drunk if they split the bottle. But if she drank it on her own . . .

"The choice is yours."

He swallowed. "You swear to me that neither of us will ever touch another drop after tonight?"

"Not another drop. Splitting this makes it official. It's a pact." She placed the bottle in his trembling hands. "It's like signing our names in blood."

"I'm only doing this to keep you from getting sick again," he said—much more to himself than to her.

"Of course you are."

Jake closed his eyes and brought the bottle to his lips.

He saw himself standing on the edge of a very steep cliff—and as the fiery liquid coursed down his throat, filling the pit of his stomach with that warm, familiar numbness, he imagined that he could just barely see his brother Wade standing far below, shaking his head.

Eighteen

Zoey lay in bed, staring despondently at her clock. It was almost nine o'clock, and Lucas still hadn't called her back. She knew he was home; she'd seen him helping his father take the Christmas tree off the top of the car. What was his problem? *She'd* made the first move toward making up. He couldn't have been *that* mad.

A knock on the door caused her to leap out of bed like a jack-in-the-box. For a split second she felt a fleeting sense of shame for being so eager, but she shrugged it off. The daylong, self-imposed isolation was making her seriously depressed. At this point, even fighting with Lucas would be preferable to spending any more time alone.

She threw the door open—and gasped. "Aaron!"

"Hey, Zoey."

"Aaron, I—"

He stood there in a leather jacket, looking sheepish, avoiding her eyes. Melting snowflakes covered his brown hair. "Look, I got your note and everything, but I just had to see you one last time."

She nodded, momentarily speechless.

"Is it all right if I come in?"

"Uh . . . sure," she said. She stepped aside and closed the door behind him.

"I know you're probably mad that I came over." He glanced awkwardly around her room. "I just wanted you to have something."

She shook her head. "Wanted me to have something?" she repeated inanely.

"Yeah." He reached into his jacket pocket and pulled out a cassette case. "It's nothing much . . . just some songs I recorded this past week." He handed her the case. "A couple of them are for you."

"For me?" She stared down at the label. In neat, small letters were written the words *Songs for Zoey*. She looked back into his hazel eyes. "I . . . um . . . thank you."

Aaron shrugged. "Don't thank me yet," he said. He grinned. "You haven't listened to it."

"I'm sure—I'm sure I'll love it."

He nodded. The two of them stood for a moment in silence. She still couldn't believe he'd just walked in like that, out of the blue. "Well, I guess I'd better be going," he said finally. "I'll see you around. Oh, by the way—tell Benjamin that he has great taste in music. He just let me check out all his CDs." Aaron turned toward the door and put his hand on the knob.

"Wait!" she said. "I mean—uh, why don't you stay while I listen to the tape? That way you can, you know, explain . . . I mean, you can tell me about the songs."

He smiled at her over his shoulder. "I don't know if that's such a great idea."

She shook her head. All at once she felt very calm and sure of herself. Why was she getting so worked up? So he was probably the best-looking boy in New

England. It didn't matter. She marched over to her boom box, took the tape out of the case, and slipped it into her cassette player. "Just the first couple of songs."

"Well . . . okay."

She pressed the play button, keeping her back to him. After a few seconds there was a harsh, fumbling noise, followed by the slow, melodic strains of a guitar being finger-picked. She was stunned. The music was beautiful: very sweet and complex, but not at all sappy or pretentious. It was amazing.

"*You* did this?" she said out loud.

"There aren't any words or anything," he said quickly, as if he needed to offer an excuse.

She shook her head again and turned to face him. "It's beautiful, Aaron. I—I don't know what to say."

"I'm glad you like it."

"I love it."

He looked away again. "Well . . . take it easy."

"Aaron . . ." Before she could finish, she had rushed across the room and kissed him passionately.

Aisha

What is my deepest, darkest secret? I'm not sure I have one. Well, that's not quite true: nobody except Nina and Loey knows that I lost my virginity to Jeff Pullings. I haven't told Christopher yet, but I'm sure I will, when the time is right. I don't know when that time will come. But I think sooner, rather than later.

I guess it's also a secret that I think a lot about my race. I mean, nobody else on Chatham Island seems to think about it at all. A large part of why I initially resisted Christopher was because he's African-American. It seemed a little too convenient that the only two black kids on the island should get together. I do have to admit now that I'm very glad I gave up trying to resist him. African-American or not, he seems like the one for me — at least for now.

I'm not quite sure why I've been thinking so much about my race recently. It could be just that I'm getting older and I'm trying to figure out what it means to be an African American woman in this day and age. In the past three years I haven't had much exposure to any kind of racism, with the obvious exception of what happened with those skinheads. I _know_ racism is still alive and well in America. Living on Chatham Island sometimes makes it easy to forget. And I don't know if that's such a good thing.

I guess my real secret is that I want to escape and experience life to the fullest. I've been too sheltered for too long. College is just around the corner, and I can't wait. I'm thinking BU, so I can be in Boston— which isn't too far from home. Just far enough so I can get out and prove to the world that an African American woman can accomplish anything she wants.

Nineteen

Aisha took one last bite of pasta, then put her fork down and sighed happily. The entire night had been unreal. Ever since Christopher had arrived at her house, she'd been feeling as if she'd been magically transported into some old Humphrey Bogart movie. She stared across the table at Christopher—who, in his dark suit, was looking more handsome then Denzel Washington and Wesley Snipes *combined*—then over his shoulder and out the big window, where the lights on Chatham, Penobscot, and Allworthy islands glittered like distant stars across the snowy bay. It was like a dream.

"What are you thinking?" Christopher asked softly.

"I'm thinking that you should feel free to surprise me like this anytime you want."

He smiled. "I'm glad. Have I mentioned yet that you look incredibly beautiful?"

"About a dozen times, but don't let that stop you."

"It won't."

Even Aisha had to admit that she *did* look good that night. Her mom had lent her an elegant, strapless black dress that Mrs. Gray had worn long ago—back when she'd been barely older than Aisha herself—and it fit perfectly.

"So what's the big surprise?" she asked while the waiter cleared their plates. "Does it have anything to do with why you sold your car?"

"Sort of." Christopher waited until the waiter was gone and they were all alone again. He put his arms on the table, then leaned forward and looked her in the eye. "Aisha, I'm leaving Chatham Island."

"*What?*" Suddenly she felt ill. "*When?*"

"Sometime in January." He took her hands, which were now cold and clammy. "I'm joining the army."

"The army?" She shook her head uncomprehendingly. "Why—why would you want to do something like that?"

"Because I need to make some changes in my life, Eesh. There's nothing for me on Chatham Island except a few dead-end jobs that are bound to dry up." His tone was grave. "Some of them already have. I can't afford to live on the island anymore."

"Well, what about . . . your *life?*" she asked. "I mean, your whole life is there." She squeezed his hands. "*I'm* there. Can't you find some kind of job here in Weymouth or something?"

"It would all be the same, Eesh," he said. "Nothing that leads to any kind of future. I want all the things you want: college, a good career, a nice house—the works. The only way I can possibly get enough money for college is by joining the army."

She kept shaking her head. "But there has to be some other way. . . ."

"You're making it sound like joining the army is like going to jail or something," he said with a laugh. "It's gonna be great. I get to travel, and learn all kinds

171

of new things, and get in really great shape. Think about it.'' He brought his face closer to hers, obviously in an effort to be convincing. ''It's the perfect decision for me.''

Aisha felt as if all the pleasure she'd experienced that night had somehow been released, like air out of a balloon. *This* was the surprise he'd been keeping— that he would be leaving to join the army? She blinked rapidly, feeling hot tears welling in the corners of her eyes.

''Eesh, please, don't cry,'' he begged. ''We're here to celebrate.''

''Celebrate?'' She sniffed, pulling her hands from his and jamming them into her purse for some tissues. ''Celebrate that as of January, I'm never gonna see you again?''

He smiled. ''That's not true,'' he said in a soothing voice. ''We're never going to be apart, ever.''

''What do you mean?'' She wiped her eyes. ''Is the army setting up some kind of new base on Chatham Island?''

''No, no, nothing like that. But my decision to join the army is only half the surprise.''

Aisha took the tissue away from her face—then froze. While her eyes had been closed, Christopher had put something on the table. It was a small, square velvet box—the kind of box meant for holding a ring. Her pulse snapped into overdrive.

''What . . . what's that?'' she choked.

Christopher leaned forward again. His beautiful dark eyes stared deeply into hers. ''Aisha . . . ever since you came after me that day to save my life, I knew there was no one in the world for me besides you. It's true. Every morning when I wake up, I feel like the luckiest man alive. I don't know anyone sweeter, smarter, more caring, or more beautiful than you are. And that's why I want us to be together forever.''

He paused, then opened the box, revealing a sparkling silver ring.

''Aisha Gray, will you marry me?''

Claire

My deepest, darkest secret? I suppose, it changes from day to day. A person's own secrets depend largely on what other people are thinking and what their secrets may be.

For instance, I have a strong suspicion that Nina lost her virginity to Benjamin when they went to Boston. I have no way of knowing for sure; neither of them will tell me, of course. But I also know that until very recently, Nina thought that I <u>wasn't</u> a virgin.

So now one of my deep, dark secrets is that I really am.

That probably won't be a secret for long.

Another secret is that I think I'd like to fool around with Aaron Mendel. This is a problem for two reasons: one, because he seems to be infatuated with Zoey, and two, because he may very well become my stepbrother. Didn't Jane Austen once address that issue? Oh, another problem is that if I'm to have any hope of seducing Aaron, apparently I'm going to have to start reading a lot more.

All of these secrets are relatively trivial in the long run.

I guess that my deepest, darkest secret, or at least the one that is most frightening to me, is that I don't think I'm a very good person at heart.

Of course, a lot of people will tell you that's not a secret.

Twenty

Snowstorms were undeniably romantic; even Claire could appreciate that fact. As she hiked up Climbing Way toward the Grays' house, she knew that any added touch of romance would be to her advantage. Luck was on her side; she could feel it. It was a perfect night for snuggling indoors.

Sarah would arrive at her house any minute to do precisely that with Claire's father. And that meant Aaron would be all alone in his room, just waiting for something magical to happen.

Like a visit from a beautiful, single girl.

She squinted through the driving snow at the lights of the house. It looked as if Aaron's room was dark. That wasn't a very good sign. She frowned, picking up her pace. Maybe he was in his mother's room— or downstairs.

When she reached for the doorknob, the door swung open.

It was Ms. Mendel.

"Claire!" she exclaimed. She was all bundled up— obviously just leaving to go to the Geigers' house. "What a coincidence! I'm going to see your father right now."

"That's nice," Claire said, smiling politely. "I was actually dropping by to see if Aaron was around. I thought he could use some company."

"Well, aren't you a dear!" she cried, putting her hand on Claire's arm. It was all Claire could do to keep from snickering. "But Aaron's not here right now."

"He's not?"

"No. He told me he was off to visit Zoey Passmore. He left not too long ago." She lowered her voice. "I think it's so nice how you island kids are reaching out to Aaron. I know he appreciates it so much. . . ."

But Claire wasn't listening. Aaron was off to visit Zoey? This was an intolerable situation. Claire summoned all her concentration to keep her face blank, but her breath started coming fast.

". . . you all right?"

"Fine, yes," Claire said, forcing herself to smile into Sarah's puzzled face. "Sorry. I just forgot something. You'll have to excuse me. I need to make a phone call."

"Why don't you use my phone, dear?" she said. "I hope it's not anything serious."

"No, no," she lied. It *was* serious, but in no way this birdbrain could understand. "Thank you; if I could use your phone, that would be nice."

"Go on up and help yourself. First room on your left," she said as she walked out the door. "Just close the door on the way out."

"Thank you." Claire could feel her smile fizzling. "I'll probably see you later."

"Good-bye." Sarah shut the front door behind her.

Claire stormed through the foyer and up the stairs.

No, this situation wasn't going to continue. Zoey Passmore was no longer going to interfere with her plans. The time had come to use the information she had about Zoey and Aaron. After all, Lucas had a right to know that his girlfriend was being unfaithful, didn't he? And besides, Aaron might take advantage of Zoey.

"Lucas, phone for you," his mother called from downstairs.

Lucas grinned. Well, it was about time. The waiting had finally driven Zoey crazy. It had driven *him* crazy, too—but she'd caved in first. This was a major victory. He'd have the courtesy not to gloat . . . at least not right away. He picked up the phone. "Got it, Mom," he said. There was a click as she hung up. "Hello?"

"Lucas, it's Claire."

His heart sank. "Claire?"

"Well, you certainly know how to make a girl feel good about herself," she said briskly. "I don't think I've ever heard so much disappointment packed into a single syllable."

Lucas sighed. She was right; he *was* disappointed—and dealing with her mind games was the last thing he wanted to do at that moment. "Sorry," he said. "I was expecting someone else."

"Zoey, maybe?"

"How'd you guess?"

"Are you two still in some kind of a fight?" she asked.

Lucas frowned. "I really don't know if that's any of your business, Claire. Why are you calling me, anyway? I'm sure it's not to chat about the weather."

"That's what I like about you, Lucas—you always cut to the chase. No, I'm not calling about the weather. I just thought you should know that Zoey has been engaged in some extracurricular activities."

Sour bile rose in Lucas's throat. "What are you talking about?" he whispered fiercely.

"I'm talking about how your girlfriend seems to have become smitten with my potential stepbrother."

"Aaron?" Lucas barked.

"The same," Claire responded coolly. "The one who was so interested in making conversation with her at our party a few weeks ago. The one who looks like a model. The one who's with Zoey right now."

His eyes narrowed. "You're lying."

"Go see for yourself." Her tone was carefree and nonchalant. "They're at the Passmores'."

Lucas dropped the receiver on the hook and dashed downstairs.

"Lucas?" his father asked as Lucas ripped his coat out of the hall closet and threw the front door open. "Lucas!" his father yelled. "Where are you—"

Lucas shut the door and began sprinting down the road, his boots crunching loudly in the snow. *This can't be happening*, he said to himself. *She wouldn't cheat on me. Claire must be lying—setting me up for some reason.*

He nearly skidded out of control as he rounded the corner onto South Street. He could see now that the light was off in Zoey's room. Relief flashed through his brain: At least they weren't alone in her room. Maybe Aaron had come to visit her, but if he had, they were downstairs. Maybe he'd stopped by to hang out with Benjamin. Anything was possible.

The last few yards to her house seemed endless.

Finally he reached the front walk and breathlessly pounded on the door.

"Coming, Lucas," Benjamin called. He opened the door. "How's it going?"

"Is Zoey here?" he demanded, gasping for air.

"Uh, yeah," he said, clearly taken aback by Lucas's rudeness. "She's upstairs. That guy Aaron is up there, too."

"*Upstairs?* Are you sure?"

Benjamin swallowed. "I think so. Lucas, what's going—"

But Lucas was already bounding up the steps. Without pausing to knock, he threw the door open and turned on the light, his eyes blazing.

"Lucas!" Zoey whispered, horrified.

She was lying on top of the bed—her shirt partly unbuttoned, her face flushed, her hair in disarray.

And lying next to her, wearing the same wide-eyed expression of pure guilt, was Aaron Mendel.

Making Out:
Ben Takes a Chance

Book II in the explosive series about broken hearts, secrets, friendship, and of course, love.

Aisha found out first and she told **Nina,** who had to tell **Zoey,** who let it slip to **Lucas.** Now **Ben's** big secret isn't a secret any more and they're all waiting to see what happens when...

Ben
takes
a chance

Avon Flare Presents
Powerful Novels
from Award-winning Authors

Joyce Carol Thomas

Bright Shadow   84509-1/$4.50 US/$6.50 Can
Marked by Fire   79327-X/$4.50 US/$6.50 Can

Alice Childress

A Hero Ain't Nothing But a Sandwich
     00312-2/$4.50 US/$5.99 Can
Rainbow Jordan   58974-5/$4.50 US/$5.99 Can

Virginia Hamilton

Sweet Whispers, Brother Rush
     65193-9/$4.99 US/$6.50 Can

Theodore Taylor

The Cay   01003-8/$4.50 US/$5.99 Can
Sniper   71193-1/$4.50 US/$5.99 Can
The Weirdo   72017-5/$4.50 US/$6.50 Can
Timothy of the Cay   72119-8/$4.50 US/$5.99 Can

Gripping, true-life accounts
for today's teens

Edited by
Beatrice Sparks, Ph.D.

IT HAPPENED TO NANCY
She thought she'd found love...
but instead lost her life to AIDS.
77315-5/$4.99 US/$6.99 Can

ALMOST LOST
The True Story
of an Anonymous Teenager's
Life on the Streets
782841-X/$4.99 US/$6.99 Can

ANNIE'S BABY
The Diary of Anonymous,
A Pregnant Teenager
79141-2/$4.99 US/$6.99 Can

Historical Adventure and Romance with the AMERICAN DREAMS Series from Avon Flare

PLAINSONG FOR CAITLIN
by Elizabeth M. Rees   78216-2/$3.99 US/$5.50 Can
Caitlin's heart belonged to the American West . . . and the man who taught her to love it.

INTO THE WIND
by Jean Ferris   78198-0/$3.99 US/$5.50 Can
Nowhere in her dreams did Rosie imagine sailing the high seas on a pirate ship!

SONG OF THE SEA
by Jean Ferris   78199-9/$3.99 US/$5.50 Can
Together Rosie and Raider challenge the dangers of uncharted waters and unfulfilled dreams.

WEATHER THE STORM
by Jean Ferris   78198-0/$3.99 US/$4.99 Can
Fate conspired to keep Rosie and Raider apart, yet their love was even more powerful.